RUSSIAN HUMOROUS STORIES

Companion Volume
TALES FROM GOGOL
Edited by Janko Lavrin

RUSSIAN

Humorous Stories

Edited and Introduced by
JANKO LAVRIN

With drawings by George Downs

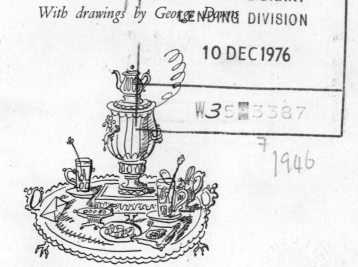

SYLVAN PRESS LONDON

THE TRANSLATORS

Of the stories in this collection, many of which now appear in English for the first time, Walter Morison has translated *The Crocodile, The Flea, The King, The Safety-Match* and *The Undertaker;* E. M. Walton: *The Discerning Dog, The Ideals of a Carp* and *In Hospital;* C. J. Lane: *Columbus Reaches the Shore;* Roza Portnova: *The Nose;* and D. J. Campbell: *The Orator.*

FIRST PUBLISHED IN 1946 BY THE SYLVAN PRESS LTD., 24, MUSEUM ST., LONDON, W.1. PRINTED BY THE WELBECSON PRESS LTD., AND BOUND BY NOVELLO & CO., LTD., LONDON
MADE IN GREAT BRITAIN

CONTENTS

INTRODUCTION

ONE still hears occasionally the old prejudice that Russia is a land without humour and that the Russians themselves are a rather solemn if not gloomy people. But nothing is wider from the mark. Like the English, the Russians too are endowed with a strong sense of humour, which they express in their own way.

An Englishman's humour, apart from stimulating his good cheer, is above all one of genial and benevolent sociability. When he jokes, he does so largely in order to forget for a while his inhibitions, his shyness and his chilly self-consciousness. All he wants is to feel at ease with his fellow-beings and to make them feel at ease with him—without any commitments on either side. Accustomed to greater security and stability than any Continental, an Englishman has comparatively few causes for that vitriolic indignation which can make one's laughter so grim and raucous. And even when he is satirical, he still balances his strong sense of proportion with his irony and remains an incorrigible optimist, devoid either of rancour or personal malice. On the other hand, such a disposition may become a weakness when turned into what might be called "boy-scout optimism," with its tendency to ignore or else to by-pass the tragic side of existence. It is precisely in the tacit acceptance of this tragic element that Russian humour seems to differ from English humour.

An average Russian, unlike an average Englishman, has always lived under the duress of such historical conditions as were bound to keep him in a rather close touch with the tragic realities of life, whether he liked it or not. Hence one of the most conspicuous features of his humour is the tendency to laugh away the sinister reality by making it look grotesquely absurd and certainly much more ludicrous than amusing. The distinction between humour and exaggerating satire has thus become on the whole smaller in Russia than it is in England, where the art of humorous understatement provides the key to the national character itself. And as far as literature is concerned, we should bear in mind that, thanks to vigilant censorship, the Russian authors were often compelled to ventilate—in the disguise of humour—such moods as in freer countries would have found an outlet in journalism or in polemics. This explains their frequent "laughter through tears." Yet when dealing with the foibles of ordinary human beings, the humorous banter of the Russians often combines kindliness and sympathy with that peculiar lack of respect for man as he is, which has been partly responsible for the "daring" psychological inquisitiveness of so many Russian authors.

All statements and generalisations of this kind are of course only approximate and should be taken with due reserve, especially when dealing with such an elusive phenomenon as national humour. But a more reliable method consists in showing a number of concrete examples, taken from literature, of how a nation laughs. Such, at any rate, is the leading idea behind this volume of Russian humorous and satirical stories from Pushkin and Gogol to our own days.

II

Strangely enough, the two principal originators of modern Russian literature, Pushkin and Gogol, differ as much in their humour as they do in their style and temperament. In spite of his trials and tribulations, which led to an untimely death, Alexander Pushkin (1799-1837) felt so much at home in this world that he could afford not only to laugh merrily, but also to smile (which, in literature, is more rare). His smile enlivens the character of "the late Ivan Petrovich Belkin"—the supposed narrator of the now famous five *Stories by Belkin*. Belkin as portrayed by Pushkin represents a truly Russian mixture of comedy and pathos, and at least two stories, ascribed to him by their author, are full of delightful humour. *The Undertaker,* with which this volume opens, is in addition a hilarious skit on the macabre genre so popular in the heyday of romanticism.

If we pass from the classical realism of Pushkin to Nikolai Gogol (1809-52), we come into touch with an uprooted romantic, who never felt quite at home in this world and was in fact frightened of it. Even the humour of his first collection of stories, *The Evenings on a Farm near Dikanka,* was essentially an escape from reality into a world of fantasy and laughter. But since reality could not be warded off, Gogol tried to disarm it by making it look as ridiculous as possible. His very "realism" consisted of a rancorous and at the same time comic exaggeration of all that is vulgar and negative in life, as we can gather from his comedy *The Inspector General,* and even more from his famous novel—*Dead Souls.* Gogol's laughter thus became particularly loud when he wanted to drown in it his own fear of life, as well as his tedium.

His grotesque fantasy, *The Nose,* which is included in this volume, is one of his Petersburg stories. But in contrast to *The Cloak, The Nevsky Prospect, A Portrait* and *The Notes of a Madman,* Gogol here presents the reader, not with a straightforward narrative, but with a transposed dream in which there is no line of demarcation between fancy and reality; in which all logic, all proportions are deliberately distorted, and therefore everything is possible, as in *Alice in Wonderland.*

Having vanished from its possessor's face, the nose actually becomes an independent person and drives in its own carriage about the Petersburg streets without condescending to acknowledge any acquaintanceship with its rightful owner, who just then is on the look-out for a suitable bride. This weird but amusing fantasy reflects some of its author's " complexes " and, like an authentic dream, provides us with a clue to one or two intimate secrets of Gogol himself.

III

The spiteful ironical attitude towards the world, expressed in Gogol's laughter, was transmitted to quite a number of Russian authors, notably to Saltykov-Shchedrin. Mikhail Saltykov-Shchedrin (1826-89), known as the author of the great but gloomy novel, *The Golovlyov Family*, was endowed with a temperament not unlike that of Swift. He adopted the loud and bitter laughter of Gogol in order to satirise the whole of Russian life, which he did in a number of narratives, especially in his history of the imaginary town of Glupov (Stupidville). Unfortunately, Saltykov-Shchedrin too often failed to separate literature from pamphleteering—with the result that a number of his brilliant writings are now dated for the very reason that they were so topical at the moment of their appearance. He was a past master of sarcastic inflection; and, anxious to elude the vigilance of the censors, it was he in particular who practised the kind of " Aesop's language " as exemplified by *The Ideals of a Carp* in this volume. This satirical fable refers to those quixotic idealists from among the Russian intelligentsia whose benevolence marked them out as victims of the much too " realistic " reactionary bureaucracy, and the latter was of course beyond good and evil.

An entirely different kind of laughter is to be found, however, in Saltykov-Shchedrin's contemporary, Nikolai Leskov (1831-95). His voluminous anti-radical novels are no longer read. His stories, on the other hand, especially those told in the style and language of the people, have comparatively recently obtained the appreciation they deserve. Leskov himself was rooted in the Russian soil and traditions, from which he derived both the substance and the inspiration for his work. As a story-teller, he was at his best in the so-called *skaz:*

the type of tale which renders the language, the style and even the inflection of the supposed narrator—usually a lower middle-class person. In such masterpieces as *The Enchanted Wanderer* and *The Sealed Angel* he achieved artistic perfection. The same can be said of the humorous *Flea,* which is included in the present volume. This typical *skaz* is, moreover, of great interest to the English readers in so far as it illustrates the attitude of the Russian simple folk towards England and the English—an attitude prompted by sympathy and the right kind of intuition. The manner in which the folk-mind (as reproduced by Leskov) throws the blame for Russia's defeat in the Crimean Campaign exclusively on the stupid authorities is as naive as it is ingenious. Another of its remarkable features is the absence of any animosity towards the victors. On the contrary, the narrator genuinely admires the English, even when, as a Russian, he refuses to capitulate before their inventiveness. The story is an example of individual humorous creation on the plane of the folk-mind and, with all its satirical hints, radiates the geniality of its author.

IV

It would be a grateful task to explore the humorous and satirical elements in the works of such writers as Turgenev, Tolstoy and Dostoevsky, but for lack of space we must limit ourselves only to Dostoevsky. Fyodor Dostoevsky (1821-81) inherited the agitated style and the tendency towards grotesque exaggerations from Gogol. At the same time he intensified the pathetic-comic type as represented by Pushkin's Belkin. Yet whatever he took on, he permeated it with his own unique temperament and personality, both of which come out in his uproarious fantasy *The Crocodile,* printed in this volume.

In order to understand this " unusual occurrence," the reader should know something about the background of the 'sixties, in the middle of which *The Crocodile* was written. For those were the years not only of great reforms initiated by the abolition of serfdom in 1861, but also of a gradual industrialisation and capitalisation of Russia—a process in which the "enlightened" if not exactly disinterested foreigners took a prominent part. Advanced Western political and scientific ideas were greeted by the Russian intellectuals with all the greater enthusiasm because for them such ideas were still forbidden fruit. So among the less discriminating rank and file of the radicals there must have been quite a few of those camp-followers and "flunkeys of ideas," whom Dostoevsky repeatedly portrayed in his novels, the nastiest of them all being the portrait of Rakitin in *Brothers Karamazov*. But the brainless and obtuse bureaucracy of the old conservative type still lingered on, often surrounded by the equally brainless careerists and windbags flirting with the progressive younger generation.

Dostoevsky evidently wanted to deliver a blow at all this by means of his laughter. So he invented the "unusual" situation in which a crocodile on show swallows such a windbag, whose "enlightened" reactions in the crocodile's interior are duly reported to the readers. His frustrated vanity is at last gratified, since his case is being talked about, discussed in the newspapers, and watched by thousands of spectators whose entrance fees liberally flow into the pocket of the enterprising owner of the crocodile. But the story speaks for itself, and so it hardly requires any further comments and elucidations.

While passing from Dostoevsky to Anton Chekhov (1860-1904), we leave the age of monumental Russian realism behind and begin to watch the gradual though interesting process of its disintegration. Yet the continuity of tradition remained. The early period of Chekhov shows quite a few links with Gogol, or rather with the peculiar laughter of Gogol. At that time he was still a student of medicine in Moscow, and his humorous pot-boilers were full of amusing skits and situations, as we

can see from *The Orator* and *The Safety-Match* (included
in this collection)—both of them dating from that period.

The first of them represents just a funny situation for
its own sake, with a dig or two at the bribe-taking official-
dom, as well as at the frowsy background of a provincial
existence. *The Safety-Match,* on the other hand, reads
like a hilarious parody on detective stories. Although the
author was only twenty-four when he wrote it (1884), his
skill in handling the plot and the satire is quite remarkable. It was only after 1885 that Chekhov's laughter
became replaced by that nostalgic sadness, the " atmos-
phere " of which prevails in his later works. But even
these are not devoid of humorous touches, which are also
found in his plays.

There were of course several other humorists in that
otherwise gloomy era, such as Leikin, or the talented
diseur Gorbunov—the creator of the Russian counterpart
of Colonel Blimp. Even when the Chekhov period
was replaced by modernism, neither its " ivory towers "
nor its solemn highbrow character precluded it from
humour.

V

The symbolist movement, which marked the height of
Russian modernism, gave a number of caustic comments
upon life, such as Blok's play, *A Puppet Show,* in which
there is more despair than laughter. On the other hand,
the average readers were content with much lighter
humorous fare. This was provided by the authors,
gathered round the periodical *Satiricon,* in which the
sketches by Arkady Averchenko were conspicuous during
the years preceding the first World War and the Revolution of 1917.

The Revolution was too serious an affair for humour
to be indulged in for its own sake, but it provided much
scope for political and social lampoons. When, after the
cataclysm, it was possible to print books once again, the
bulk of them dealt with the heroic and romantic side of

the Revolution on the one hand, and with the building up of a new world on the other. But room was now made also for humour and satire. One of the most outstanding satirical works to be published soon after the civil war was Ilya Ehrenburg's (b. 1889) *Extraordinary Adventures of Julio Jurenito,* with its Swift-like jeering at the entire capitalistic civilisation and, as far as possible, even at the aftermath of the Revolution itself.

Both humour and satire can be found in the incisive yet detached realism of Isaac Babel (b. 1894). Born in Odessa into a Jewish family, he started his literary career in 1915 with sketches from Jewish life in his native town. Fame came to him only after the Revolution, when his incredibly detached and concentrated snapshots of Budyonny's famous red cavalry in its fight against the Poles appeared. The story we have included in this volume is taken, however, from his tales of the Jewish underworld in Odessa, with its " king " Benya Krik skilfully depicted in all his grandeur. Babel's humour is caustic and often cruel—quite in the style of the finale of this story. On the other hand, his twinkle comes out also in his renderings of the linguistic peculiarities of the Jewish community he describes, and these are untranslatable.

VI

Further opportunities for humorous satire were provided by the NEP period of Soviet Russia, during which her population was anxious to settle down amidst all the duress and confusion. That period found a many-sided reflection in literature, and for the first time since the Revolution the country was able to laugh at itself with a good conscience. The number of humorous and satirical authors was on the increase, but we must limit ourselves only to three conspicuous names—Zoshchenko, Ilf and Petrov.

Mikhail Zoshchenko's (b. 1895) principal genre is the humorous anecdote in the form of a *skaz,* inherited from

Leskov. His supposed narrator is always a lower middle-class person whose slang and inflections the author uses dexterously and with his tongue in his cheek. His sketches are an amusing encyclopaedia of everyday life in Soviet Russia, as seen in a slightly crooked mirror. There is a mistaken notion abroad that the Soviet authors have not the freedom to criticise conditions in their own country. Judging by Zoshchenko's two stories in this volume, they are certainly allowed to ridicule, even to the point of exaggerated parody, the things that ought to be and could be improved. Were this not so, Zoshchenko's works would hardly be printed by the State Publishing Company on the terms of a best seller.

Ilya Ilf (1897-1940) made—in collaboration with Evgeny Petrov*—a great hit with the humorously picaresque novels, *The Twelve Chairs* and *The Little Golden Calf*. The actual hero of both of them is the new profiteer, Ostap Bender, produced by the Soviet conditions and magnificently portrayed against the background of the NEP. Resourceful and generous, he is of a brand similar to that of Babel's Benya Krik, but his field of activities is much wider. It is in fact provided almost by the whole of the Soviet Russia, which the two authors depict with plenty of cheerful and ironical laughter. As though anxious to extend their laughter even beyond Russia, they travelled to the United States and gave an amusing account of their impressions in their book, *Little Golden America*. But if the reader wants to obtain a tabloid sample of their art he can find it in *Columbus Reaches the Shore,* with which we suitably conclude the present volume.

It would be presumptuous to regard this collection as anything more than an introduction to the subject. Its aim is to give the non-Russian reader at least a foretaste of how Russia laughs and how this laughter is expressed in her literature.

* Killed in the fighting for Sebastopol.

ALEXANDER PUSHKIN

THE UNDERTAKER

Do we not coffins every day behold,
The greyness of a world that's growing old?
DERZHAVIN

THE LAST GOODS and chattels of Hadrian Prokhorov the undertaker were piled on a hearse, and for the fourth and final time the two thin nags tottered from Basmannaya Street to Nikitskaya Street, whither the undertaker was moving with all his household. Locking up his old shop, he nailed to the door an announcement that the house was for sale or to let and set out on foot for his new abode. As he drew near to the little yellow house that had so long ago taken his fancy and which he had now purchased for a fairly considerable sum, the old undertaker felt to his surprise that there was no gladness in his heart. Crossing the unfamiliar threshold and finding everything upside down in his new dwelling, he sighed for the old place where for eighteen years everything had been kept in the strictest order; he began to scold his two daughters and the female help for their tardiness, and himself set about lending them a hand. Soon order was established; the ikon-case, the dresser, the table, the sofa and the bed occupied their appointed corners in the back room; in the kitchen and the parlour were set the attributes of the master's calling: coffins of every size and colour, and cupboards with mourning hats, capes and tapers. Above the door there now hung a sign representing a corpulent Cupid holding a torch upside down, with the inscription "Here are sold and lined plain and painted coffins; also let out for hire, and old ones patched up." The girls withdrew to their chamber; Hadrian went the rounds of his new home, sat down by the window and ordered the samovar to be prepared.

The enlightened reader will know that Shakespeare and Walter Scott both represented their grave-diggers as cheerful and jocund individuals, seeking to startle our imaginations with this incongruity. Our respect for the truth prevents us from following their example, and we are bound to confess that the nature of our undertaker completely corresponded to his sombre calling. Hadrian Prokhorov was as a rule gloomy and pensive. He scarcely ever broke his silence save to upbraid his daughters when he found them idly peeping out at those passing the window, or to screw a higher price for his wares from those who were so unfortunate (and sometimes so fortunate) as to require them. And so Hadrian, sitting at the window and sipping his seventh cup of tea, was, as usual, plunged in melancholy thoughts. He thought of the pouring rain that a week before had swamped the funeral of a retired brigadier ere it got outside the town; many capes had shrunk in consequence, many hats had warped; he could see that he was in for a considerable amount of expense, for the stock of funeral deckings that had served him so long and so well had been reduced to a pitiable condition. He hoped that he might be able to recover his losses on the old widow of the merchant Tryukhin, who for over a year had lain at death's door. But Tryukhina was passing away on Razgulyay Street, and Prokhorov feared that her heirs, despite their promise, might draw the line at sending for him now that he lived so far away, and come to terms with a more readily accessible undertaker.

These ponderings were interrupted by three Masonic taps on the door. "Who is it?" asked Hadrian. The door opened, and an individual in whom at the first glance it was possible to recognise a German artisan entered the room and cheerfully approached the undertaker. "Pardon me, my dear neighbour," he said, in that variety of Russian which to this day we are unable to hear without a smile; " pardon me for intruding. I was

anxious to make your acquaintance without delay. I am
a shoemaker, and my name is Schulz, Gottlieb Schulz,
and I live across the way from you, in that little house
you can see from your window. Tomorrow I am celebrating my silver wedding, and I have much pleasure in
inviting you and your daughters to dinner." The invitation was graciously accepted. The undertaker asked the
shoemaker to sit down and take a dish of tea, and thanks
to Gottlieb Schulz's frank nature they were soon engaged
in amicable converse. "And how is business?" asked
Hadrian.—"So-so," replied Schulz; "I can't really com-
plain. Though of course my goods are different from
yours; a live man can manage without shoes, but a dead
man must have a coffin or bust."—"Very true," observed
Hadrian; "on the other hand if a live man can't afford
a pair of shoes he goes about bare-footed, but a dead
beggar gets a coffin for nothing." So their talk continued
for some time; at length the shoemaker rose and took his
leave of the undertaker, not forgetting before he left to
renew his invitation.

At noon precisely next day the undertaker and his
daughters passed through the gateway of their new home
and crossed the road to their neighbour's house. I will
not pause to describe either Hadrian Prokhorov's Russian
kaftan or his daughters' European finery, departing in
this way from the custom of contemporary novelists.
However, I think it worth mentioning that Darya and
Akulina had put on their yellow bonnets and their red
shoes, which occurred only on very special occasions.

The shoemaker's pokey quarters were chock-full of
guests, most of them German craftsmen with their better
halves and their apprentices. The Russian element was
represented by the Finnish night-watchman Yurko, who
despite his humble calling had gained his host's particular
favour. For some twenty-five years he had kept his
nocturnal watch faithfully and truly, like Pogorelsky's
postillion. The fire of 1812, which had destroyed

B

Moscow, had also consumed his yellow sentry-box; but no sooner had the foe been driven out than it was replaced by a new one, gray, with little white columns of the Doric order, and Yurko had resumed his patrols in its vicinity girt with his axe and wearing his fustian armour. He was known to most of the Germans living by the Nikitsky Gate, some of whom had even had occasion to pass the night of Sunday to Monday in Yurko's sentry-box. Hadrian at once made his acquaintance, recognizing in him a man of whom sooner or later he might have need, and when they took their places for dinner he sat down next to the watchman. Herr and Frau Schulz and their seventeen-year-old daughter Lottchen both ate with their guests and helped the cook to serve the dishes. The beer flowed freely. Yurko ate enough for four; Hadrian kept pace with him; his daughters picked daintily; as time went by the German conversation grew noisier and noisier. Suddenly the host called for silence, and uncorking a tarred bottle said loudly in Russian: "To the health of my good Luise!" The so-called champagne foamed. The host tenderly kissed the pink cheeks of his forty-year-old spouse, and the guests drank boisterously to the worthy Luise's health. "To the health of my dear guests!" proposed the host, uncorking a second bottle, and his dear guests responded by emptying their glasses. Now toasts followed one another in rapid succession; they drank the health of each individual guest, they drank the health of Moscow and a round dozen German towns, they drank the health of all the guilds in general and of each one in particular, they drank the health of the master-craftsmen and the apprentices. Hadrian drank assiduously, and grew so merry that even he proposed some sort of jovial toast. Suddenly one of the guests, a fat pastry-cook, raised his glass and cried: "To the health of those for whom we work, *unsere Kundleute!*" The proposal, like all the rest, was accepted joyfully and unanimously. The guests began bowing to one another: the tailor to the shoemaker, the shoemaker to the tailor, the pastry-cook to them both, all of them to the pastry-cook, and so on and on. Amidst all these reciprocal bows Yurko turned to his neighbour and cried: "Come, old fellow, drink to the health of *your* clients!" All burst out laughing; but the undertaker felt offended, and frowned. No one noticed, however; the guests went on drinking, and the bells were ringing for evening service when they rose from the table.

The party broke up late, and most of the guests were tipsy when they set out for home. The fat pastry-cook and the book-binder, whose face might have been bound in red morocco, led Yurko off to his sentry-box, mindful of the saying "One good turn deserves another." The undertaker reached home drunk and angry. "After all," he mumbled to himself, "in what way is my calling less honourable than others? Is an undertaker blood-brother to the hangman? Why should those foreigners laugh at me? Am I some sort of buffoon? I had thought of inviting them to my house-warming, giving them a real good time, but I'm blowed if I will now! Tell you what I'll do: invite my clients, the Orthodox dead 'uns."—"God-a-mercy!" cried the female help, who was pulling off his boots. "Whatever are you saying? The idea of asking corpses to a party!"—"'Pon my word I will," went on Hadrian; "for tomorrow, too. Delighted to see you tomorrow evening, my benefactors, I'll say; come and have a good blow-out." With these words the undertaker sank on his bed and was soon snoring.

It was still dark when he was roused. The widow Tryukhina had passed away, and a messenger had come galloping on horseback with the news. The undertaker gave him ten copecks in silver as a tip, hurriedly dressed, took a cab and drove to Razgulyay Street. Policemen already stood at the deceased woman's door, and tradesmen were hovering about like crows that have scented carrion. The dead woman lay on a table, yellow as wax, but as yet untouched by corruption. Round the table crowded her heirs, her neighbours and her domestics. All the windows were open; candles were burning; priests were saying prayers. Hadrian went up to Tryukhina's nephew, a young merchant in a fashionably-cut frock-coat, and informed him that a coffin, candles, a shroud and the rest of the funeral requirements would be supplied without delay and in good order. The heir thanked him absent-mindedly, saying that expense was no object and that he left it to the undertaker's conscience. As usual the undertaker swore that he would not ask a penny more than he must, exchanged a significant glance with the head clerk and drove off to make his arrangements. All day long he was driving from Razgulyay Street to the Nikitsky Gate and back; by evening he had made all his arrangements, and dismissing his cab he set off home on foot. It was a moonlight night. The undertaker reached the Nikitsky Gate safe and sound. At the Church of the Assumption he was hailed by our friend Yurko who, recognizing the undertaker, wished him good-night. It was late. Hadrian was approaching his house when it suddenly seemed to him that someone had gone up to his gate, opened it and slipped inside. "Who can that be?" he wondered. "Does somebody else need my services? Or was it a thief? Or are those wenches of mine receiving visitors in their bedroom? Shouldn't be surprised!" And the undertaker was already thinking of summoning his friend Yurko to his assistance. At this moment another figure approached the gate and was about to enter, but on seeing the undertaker come running it halted and took off its three-cornered hat. Hadrian seemed to know the face, but in his haste he hadn't time to look at it properly. "Have you come to see me?" he panted. "Please walk in."—"Don't stand on ceremony," responded the other in a hollow voice; "you go on ahead

and show your guests the way!" Nor had Hadrian any time to stand on ceremony. He unfastened the gate and went up the stairs, the other following. It seemed to Hadrian that people were moving about in his rooms. "What the devil?" he thought to himself, and hurried in. And his legs sagged beneath him. The room was full of dead people. Through the window the moon shone on their blue and yellow faces, their sunken mouths, their dull. half-closed eyes and their pinched noses . . . . With horror Hadrian recognized in them people he had helped to bury, and the guest who had entered with him was none other than the brigadier who had been interred in the pouring rain. All of them, dead of both sexes, surrounded the undertaker with bows and greetings, all save one poor fellow who had recently had a pauper's burial and who, embarrassed, and ashamed of his ragged garments, did not approach but stood humbly in a corner. The rest were all decently dressed: the deceased ladies in laces and ribbons, the deceased officials in their uniforms, though their chins were unshaven, and the deceased merchants in their Sunday kaftans. "You see, Prokhorov," said the brigadier, speaking in the name of the whole honourable company, "we have all responded to your invitation; only those remained at home who were unable to come, such as had completely decomposed and of whom nothing remained save the bare bones; and even one of these could not resist, he was so anxious to come to your party." Here a small skeleton pushed its way through the throng and approached Hadrian. His skull grinned amiably at the undertaker. Here and there fragments of bright-green and red cloth and aged linen hung on him as on a pole, and the bones of his legs rattled in large jack-boots like pestles in mortars. "I see you don't recognize me, Prokhorov," said the skeleton. "Don't you remember the retired sergeant of the Guard, Peter Petrovich Kurilkin, to whom in 1799 you sold your first coffin, palming off pine as solid oak?" Saying this the skeleton extended a bony embrace; but Hadrian, pulling himself together, gave a cry and pushed him away. Peter Petrovich staggered, fell, and crumbled into dust. From the dead proceeded a murmur of indignation; all rose in defence of their colleague's honour and closed in on Hadrian with oaths and threats, and their poor host, dazed by their cries and almost suffocated, quite lost his head, tripped over the bones of the retired sergeant of the Guard, and lost consciousness.

The sun had long been shining on the bed upon which the undertaker lay. At last he opened his eyes and beheld the female help, who was blowing up the flame of the samover. With horror Hadrian recalled the events of the previous night. The widow Tryukhina, the briga-dier and Sergeant Kurilkin passed vaguely through his mind. He waited in silence for the servant to begin speaking and tell him the outcome of his nocturnal adventures.

"How sound you've been sleeping, Hadrian Pro-khorovich!" said Aksinya as she handed him his dressing-gown. "The tailor from next door looked in, and Yurko the night-watchman came to say that there was a party in the neighbourhood, but you were so fast asleep we didn't like to disturb you."

"And was there any message about the deceased Tryukhina?"

"Deceased? Is she dead, then?"

"Why, you stupid girl, didn't you yourself help me arrange her funeral yesterday?"

"Have you gone out of your mind, Hadrian Pro-khorovich, or is it that you haven't yet got over the effects of yesterday's drinking? Funeral indeed! Why, all day long you were making merry at the shoemaker's; came home drunk, fell into bed and been fast asleep until this minute. They've just rung for evening service."

"Is that really so?" asked the overjoyed undertaker.

"Of course it is," replied the female help.

"In that case, get busy and make me some tea. And send in those girls of mine."

NIKOLAI GOGOL

THE NOSE

ON the 25th of March an extraordinary thing happened in St. Petersburg. The barber Ivan Yakovlevitch, who lives on the Voznesiensky Prospect (his surname has been forgotten, and even on his sign-board, which depicts a gentleman with a soaped cheek and on which are inscribed the words, ". . . and blood is let," nothing else appears), barber Ivan Yakovlevitch woke early and smelled the odour of hot bread. Raising himself gently on the bed, he saw that his spouse, a respectable lady who was very fond of coffee, was taking freshly baked bread out of the oven.

"To-day, Praskovya Osipovna, I shall not drink coffee," said Ivan Yakovlevitch, "but instead I'd like some hot bread and onion." (That is, Ivan Yakovlevitch would have liked both, but he knew that it was absolutely impossible to demand both things at once, as Praskovya Osipovna did not encourage such fancies.)

"Let the fool eat the bread—suits me," thought the spouse, "there will be all the more coffee left," and she threw a loaf of black bread on the table.

For decency's sake, Ivan Yakovlevitch put on his frock-coat over his shirt and, sitting down at the table, took some salt, peeled two onions, took up a knife and, with an air of importance, began to cut the bread. Having cut the loaf in halves, he looked inside and, to his amazement, saw something white. Ivan Yakovlevitch cautiously poked the knife at it and touched it wih his finger. "It

is firm," he said to himself, "what can it be?" He
pushed his fingers in and extracted—a nose!

Ivan Yakovlevitch was confounded. He began to rub
his eyes and to feel the object. Yes, it was a nose, really a
nose! And there seemed to be something familiar
about it. Ivan Yakovlevitch's face expressed terror, but
his terror was nothing compared with the indignation
which filled his wife.

"Animal, where have you cut this nose from?" she
shouted furiously. "Crook, drunkard! I shall report
you to the police myself. Robber! I have already heard
from three people that, while shaving them, you pull
them about by their noses so much that they can hardly
stay in their seats."

But Ivan Yakovlevitch felt half dead. He realised that
the nose belonged to nobody else but the collegiate
assessor Kovalev, whom he shaved every Wednesday and
Sunday.

"Wait, Praskovya Osipovna, I'll wrap it in a little rag
and put it in a corner. Let it lie there for a little while,
and I will carry it out later on."

"I will not even hear of it. That I should allow a
sliced nose to lie in my room! Like a baked rusk! All
he knows is how to pull a razor along a strop, and he soon
won't be fit to do even that, vagabond, blockhead! Away
with it. Out! Take it wherever you wish—I won't have
it in the place for a minute."

Ivan Yakovlevitch stood as if stunned. He thought and
thought and did not know what to make of it. "The
devil knows how it happened," he said at last, scratching
behind his ear. "Can't make it out. Did I come home
drunk yesterday or not? Most likely I did, judging by
all the signs. This thing is impossible. Bread is a matter
for baking, but as far as a nose goes . . . no. Can't make
it out."

Ivan Yakovlevitch stopped talking. The thought that
a policeman might discover the nose on him and charge

him made him feel quite faint. He could already see the
blood-red collar, handsomely embroidered with silver, a
sword . . . and began to tremble. Finally he grabbed
his breeches and high boots, put all this rubbish on and,
accompanied by violent exhortations from Praskovya
Osipovna, he wrapped the nose in a rag and went out into
the street.

He wanted to push it under a loose curb stone at somebody's gate or drop it somewhere without being noticed
and then turn into a side street, but unfortunately he kept
running into some acquaintance or other who would
immediately begin asking: "Where are you going?" or
"Who have you come out to shave so early?" So that
Ivan Yakovlevitch could not possibly find an appropriate
moment. Once he managed to drop it, but a sentry
pointed with his halberd from the distance and shouted:
"You've dropped something—pick it up!" and Ivan
Yakovlevitch had to pick up the nose and hide it in his
pocket.

He became desperate, especially as the crowds continued
to increase as the stores and shops began to open. He
decided to go to the Isaaky Bridge. Perhaps he could
succeed in throwing the nose into the Neva.

But I am somewhat at fault for not having yet said anything about Ivan Yakovlevitch, an honourable man in
many respects. Ivan Yakovlevitch, like all honourable
Russian artisans, was a terrible drunkard, and, although
he shaved strange chins every day, his own was always
unshaven. Ivan Yakovlevitch's frock-coat (Ivan Yakovlevitch never wore an ordinary jacket) was piebald—that is,
it was black but dappled with brownish yellow and grey;
the collar was shiny and, in place of its three buttons,
only the threads were hanging.

Ivan Yakovlevitch was a great cynic, and, when the
collegiate assessor Kovalev used to tell him during shaving,
"Your hands, Ivan Yakovlevitch, always stink!" Ivan
Yakolevitch would answer with the question, "Why

shouldn't they stink?" " I don't know, brother, but they stink!" the collegiate assessor would reply, and Ivan Yakovlevitch, after taking a pinch of snuff, would in revenge soap Kovalev's cheek as well as under his nose, behind his ear, under his beard—in short, wherever he fancied.

This honourable citizen now found himself on the Isaaky Bridge. First he looked round, then he leaned over the parapet as if to look under the bridge and to see whether there were any fish in the river, and quietly threw in the rag containing the nose. At once he felt as if a ton weight had fallen from his shoulders. Ivan Yakovlevitch even chuckled. Instead of going to shave the chins of officials, he was departing to an establishment bearing the inscription " Food and tea " in order to obtain a glass of punch, when he suddenly noticed at the end of the bridge a police officer, of noble appearance, with broad whiskers, a three-cornered hat and a sword. He stopped dead. The police officer, however, was beckoning him with his finger and calling, " Come here, friend."

Ivan Yakovlevitch, fully aware of how a man in this uniform should be treated, took off his cap at a distance, and, approaching him nimbly, said, " Good morning, your Honour."

" No, no, brother, don't be so formal. Tell me, what were you doing there on the bridge?"

" As true as God is in Heaven, sir, I was on my way to shave somebody and only peeped at the river to see how fast it was running"

" You are lying, you are lying, brother. You will not get away with that! Kindly answer me."

" I would willingly shave your Honour twice or even three times a week," answered Ivan Yakovlevitch.

" No, my friend, that's nonsense! Three barbers attend to me already and they regard it as a great honour. Now tell me, what were you doing there?"

Ivan Yakovlevitch became pale . . .

But here the scene becomes completely obscured by mist, and we know absolutely nothing else of what transpired.

2

Collegiate assessor Kovalev awoke comparatively early and made the sound, b-r-r-r-r with his lips, which he always did on waking, although he himself did not know the reason for it. Kovalev stretched himself and called to his servant to give him a mirror which was standing on the table. He wanted to look at a pimple which had suddenly appeared on his nose the night before, but to his great amazement he saw that there was a completely smooth place instead of the nose. Kovalev grew frightened and shouted for some water. He rubbed his eyes with a towel—still no nose! He began to feel his face with his hand, and pinched himself to find out whether he was asleep or not—apparently he was not. Collegiate assessor Kovalev jumped out of bed, shook himself—still no nose! He immediately ordered his clothes to be brought to him, and rushed off straight to the Chief of Police.

But in the meantime I should say something about Kovalev, so that the reader may see what kind of a collegiate assessor he was.

It is impossible to compare collegiate assessors who attain this rank by means of a certificate of learning with those who are being turned out in the Caucasus. They are two entirely different species. Learned collegiate assessors . . . But Russia is such a peculiar country, that if you say something about one collegiate assessor, then all collegiate assessors from Riga to Kamchatka, without exception, will take it personally. The same applies to all other ranks and professions.

Kovalev was a Caucasian collegiate assessor. He had held this rank for only two years, and therefore could not forget it for a moment, and, in order to add more nobility and importance to himself, he never called himself just a collegiate assessor, but always a major. " Listen, little pigeon," he would say on meeting a woman in the street

who was selling shirt-fronts, " call at my place, my flat
is on the Sadovaya. You just ask ' Does Major Kovalev
live here?'—anybody will direct you." If, however, he
met a comely woman, he would, in addition, give her
certain secret instructions, adding, " Darling, you ask for
Major Kovalev's flat." Therefore, we too, shall in future
call him a major.

Major Kovalev was in the habit of strolling along the
Nevsky Prospect every day. The collar of his shirt-front
was always extremely clean and well starched. His side-
whiskers were of the kind which are still to be seen on
government and district land surveyors, on architects and
regimental doctors, also on those performing various duties
and, generally speaking, on all those men who have fat,
rosy cheeks and are good boston players. These side-
whiskers grow along the very middle of the cheek and go
straight up to the nose. Major Kovalev carried a multitude of little carnelian seals, some with coats of arms and
some on which were engraved " Wednesday," " Thursday," " Monday," etc. Major Kovalev had come up to
Petersburg on business, namely, to find an employment
worthy of his profession. If possible he would have liked
the post of Vice-Governor or, failing that, some executive
position in an important department. Major Kovalev
was also not averse to marriage, but only if the prospective
bride happened to have a dowry of two hundred thousand
roubles. Therefore, reader, you may judge for yourself
what the Major's predicament was when, instead of a nose,
not uncomely but of reasonable proportions, he saw a
very silly plain and smooth place.

As bad luck would have it, not one cab driver showed
himself in the street, and he had to walk, having wrapped
himself in his cloak and covered his face with a handkerchief, as if his nose was bleeding.

" But perhaps I only imagined it—it is impossible that
a nose should so stupidly disappear," he thought, and
entered a pastry shop, where he intended to look at him-

self in a mirror.

Fortunately, there was nobody there. The boys were sweeping the rooms and replacing the chairs: some of them, with sleepy eyes, were carrying trays of hot pies. Yesterday's papers, wet with coffee, were scattered on tables and chairs.

"Well, thank Heaven, nobody's here," Kovalev muttered, "I can have a look now." He timidly approached the mirror and looked into it.

"The Devil take it—what a filthy mess," he said and spat. "If there were only something in its place—but no, simply nothing there!"

He bit his lips in his grief and, on leaving the pastry shop, he decided, against his usual wont, not to look or smile at anybody.

Suddenly, as if thunderstruck, he stopped in front of a house. He beheld an inexplicable apparition. A coach stopped at the house entrance; the door opened and a gentleman in uniform jumped out and ran up the steps. How great was Kovalev's horror and at the same time his amazement when he recognised who it was—his very own nose! It seemed to him, witnessing this unusual sight, that everything swayed before him. He could hardly stand, but decided, whatever happened, to await the return of the nose to the coach. He was trembling as if with ague.

After two minutes the nose actually reappeared. It was in a uniform embroidered with gold and was wearing a stiff collar and suede breeches. A sword hung at its side. Judging by the plume on its hat, it held the rank of a State Councillor. Everything pointed to the fact that it was going to visit somebody. It looked around and, calling to the driver, "Let's go," sat down and was driven away.

Poor Kovalev nearly went mad. He did not know what to think of such a strange occurrence. How could the nose, which was yesterday on his face and could neither ride nor walk, wear a uniform? He ran after the coach,

which, unfortunately, did not go far and stopped in front
of the bazaar. He hurried there, threading his way
among a row of old beggar women, with bandaged faces
and two holes for eyes, at whom he used to laugh. The
crowd was not large. Kovalev was in such a bad state
that he could not decide anything, and his eyes were
searching for the gentleman in all the corners. Finally,
he saw it standing in front of a shop. The nose's face
was completely hidden in the large military collar and it
was examining some merchandise with deep attention.

" How is the nose to be approached?" thought Kovalev.
" Judging by everything—the uniform and the hat—it is
obvious that it is a State Councillor. The Devil knows
how it is to be done!"

Drawing nearer, Kovalev coughed, but the nose did not
change its posture for a moment.

" Sir," said Kovalev, inwardly forcing himself to some
courage, " dear sir . . ."

" What is it you wish?" answered the nose, turning
round.

" It is strange, dear sir . . . it seems to me . . . you
ought to know your place. And suddenly I find you—and
where? You will agree . . ."

" Forgive me, but I do not understand what you wish
to say. Will you kindly explain?"

" How shall I explain it?" thought Kovalev, and,
gathering courage, he began, " Of course, I . . . by the
way, I am a major. You will agree that it is unseemly
for me to walk about without a nose. Some beggar
woman selling peeled oranges on the Voskresenki Bridge
may sit there without a nose, but I have prospects of
obtaining . . . and in addition, being acquainted with
ladies in many households—Mrs. Chechtareva, State
Councillor's wife, and others . . . Judge for yourself. I
do not know, dear sir " (at this Major Kovalev shrugged
his shoulders), " forgive me, whether this is in accordance
with the rules of honour and duty. You yourself will

understand . . ."

"I do not understand anything at all," answered the nose. "Kindly explain more clearly."

"My dear sir," said Kovalev, full of dignity, "I do not know how to interpret your words. It seems to me that the whole matter is quite obvious ... or do you want ... ? After all, you are my own nose!"

The nose looked at the major and raised its eyebrows slightly.

"You are mistaken, sir, I am myself. Besides, there can be no close relationship between us. Judging by the buttons on your uniform, you are serving in a different department." Having said this, the nose turned away.

Kovalev became completely confused, not knowing what to do, nor even what to think. At that moment a pleasant rustle of female dresses was heard. An elderly lady approached, her clothes profusely trimmed with lace, and with her was a slim girl in a white dress which clung attractively to her graceful waist. She was wearing a straw-coloured hat as light as a pastry. A tall man-in-waiting stopped behind them and opened a snuff-box. He wore large side-whiskers and at least a dozen collars.

Kovalev moved nearer, pushed out the batiste collar of his shirt-front, re-arranged the seals which were hung on his gold chain, and, smiling in all directions, turned his attention to the slim lady, who, like a spring flower, was bending slightly and was holding her little white hand, with semi-transparent fingers, to her forehead. The smile on Kovalev's face broadened even more when he saw, under the hat, her round chin of lucid whiteness and part of her cheek, the shade of a rose in spring. Suddenly, however, he jumped away, as if burnt. He remembered that, instead of a nose, he had absolutely nothing at all, and tears sprang to his eyes. He turned round with the intention of telling the gentleman in uniform, quite frankly, that he was only impersonating a State Councillor—that he was a rogue and a scoundrel and was

c

nothing but his, Kovalev's, nose; but the nose was no longer there. It had had time to drive away, probably to visit somebody else.

This drove Kovalev to despair. He went back and stood still for a moment against a pillar, looking carefully in every direction to see whether he could catch sight of the nose. He clearly remembered that its hat bore a plume and that its uniform had gold embroidery, but he had not noticed either the great-coat or the colour of the coach or the horses, nor even whether there was any footman behind it and what livery he wore. Moreover, such a multitude of coaches was driving so quickly backwards and forwards that it was difficult to pick one out; and, even if he had recognised one of them, he had no means of stopping it.

The day was lovely and sunny. There were masses of people on the Nevski; a whole flowery cascade of ladies was streaming along the pavement, which stretched from the Policeiski up to the Anichkin bridge. There went his acquaintance, the Court Councillor, whom he used to call a lieutenant-colonel, especially when strangers happened to be present. There also went Yarishkin, chief of a table in the senate, his great friend, who always lost when he played boston. There went another major, who had obtained his assessorship on the Caucasus. He was waving his hand and beckoning him.

"Oh, the Devil take it!" said Kovalev. "Hey there, cabman! Drive me at once to the Chief of Police."

Kovalev sat in the carriage and kept shouting to the cabman, "Drive as fast as you can."

"Is the Chief of Police at home?" he cried as he entered the hall.

"I am afraid not," answered the porter.

"What a nuisance!"

"Yes," replied the porter, and added, "and he only left a short time ago. Had you come a minute sooner, you might have found him in."

Kovalev returned to the carriage, without removing the handkerchief from his face, and shouted in a desperate voice: " Get a move on."

" Where to? " asked the driver.

" Straight on ! "

' What do you mean, straight on ? We've got to turn here—right or left ? "

This question made Kovalev stop and think again. In his condition it behoved him to go to the police station, not because the matter directly concerned the police, but because their orders would be more quickly obeyed than those given by anyone else. It would, however, be senseless to seek satisfaction from the authorities of the place where the nose had declared it was serving, as one could see from the replies of the nose itself that it held nothing sacred and might lie as readily in that place as it had lied in assuring him that it had never met him before. Therefore, Kovalev had almost decided to order the driver to go to the police station, when the thought struck him that this rogue and scoundrel, who had behaved so dishonestly already at the first meeting, might again, conveniently making use of time, somehow slip out of town, and all the search would be in vain, and might, God forbid, last a whole month. Finally, it seemed that Heaven itself directed him. He decided to go straight to the newspaper office with a detailed description of the nose, so that anybody meeting it could immediately return it to Kovalev, or at least tell him of its abode. Therefore, having decided this, he ordered the driver to go to the newspaper office, and, during the whole of the journey, never stopped thumping the man's back with his fist and urging him on, crying, " Hurry, dastard ! Hurry, crook ! "

" I am doing my best, sir," the driver would say, shaking his head and striking the horse, whose coat was as long as a spaniel's.

At last the carriage stopped, and Kovalev, breathless, ran into the small reception room, where a grey-haired

official, wearing an old frock-coat and glasses, was sitting
at a table, with a pen in his teeth, counting copper coins.

" Who takes advertisements ? " shouted Kovalev. " Oh,
good morning."

" Good morning," said the grey-haired official, raising
his eyes for a moment and then looking down at the small
piles of money.

" I want to insert . . ."

" Excuse me, will you kindly wait a little," murmured
the official, writing a figure on a paper with his right
hand, and, with a finger of his left hand, moving a bead
on his counting board.

A footman, with gallooned livery, and of a comparatively clean appearance, denoting his employment in
an aristocratic house, stood near the table, with a note
in his hands, and deemed it appropriate to show his
sociability by saying, " Believe me, sir, the dog is not
worth eight griven. I would not have given even eight
groshi for her, but the Countess loves her—I swear she
loves her—and whoever finds her gets a hundred roubles !
It would be right to say between ourselves, that people's
tastes are incompatible. If you so desire, then keep a setter
or a poodle, and don't be sorry to give five hundred for
it—give a thousand—but then you should get a good
dog."

The respectable official listened to this with an air of
importance, and at the same time busied himself calculating the numbers of letters in the note.

A crowd of old women stood at the side, as well as
merchants' clerks and porters with notes. One announced
that a horse-driver, of sober behaviour, was free for service;
another, that a good second-hand carriage, imported from
Paris in 1814, was for sale. There was a 19-year-old servant
girl available, practised in laundry work and suitable for
other work as well; a solid droshky, with one spring missing; a young and spirited horse, dappled grey, seventeen
years old; new turnip and radish seeds from London; a

country house, with all conveniences, two stables and a site suitable for growing a fine birch or fir grove. There was also a notice to those wishing to buy old shoe-soles with an invitation to appear at the second auction every day from 8 to 3.

The room in which all this company found itself was small, and the air in it was extremely thick, but the collegiate assessor could not smell anything, as he had covered his face with a handkerchief, and because his very own nose was—Heaven knew where.

" My dear sir, permit me to ask you . . . it is very important," he said at last impatiently.

" Just a moment, a moment . . . Two roubles forty-three kopeks! . . . Just a moment . . . One rouble sixty-four kopeks! " the grey-haired gentleman was saying, thrusting the notices in the faces of the old women and the porters.

" What is it you wish? " he said at last, turning to Kovalev.

" I should like to ask . . ." Kovalev said, " a swindle, an outrage has taken place—up to now I have not been able to find out anything. I should only like to advertise that whoever will produce the dastard to me will receive an ample reward."

" May I ask your name ? "

" But why my name ? It is impossible for me to disclose it. I have many acquaintances—Chechtareva, State Councillor's wife; Pelageya Grigorievna Podtochina, Staff Officer's wife. . . They may suddenly find out! God forbid! You can simply write, a collegiate assessor—or, even better, a major."

" Has your house-servant run away ? "

" Who is talking about a house-servant ? That would not have been such an outrage! My nose . . . has run away from me! "

" Ahem! A peculiar name! And has this Mr. Nosey stolen a large sum of money from you ? "

" My nose . . . that is . . . you are thinking of something different! My nose, my own nose, disappeared—I don't know where to. Damme, are you trying to joke with me ? "

" But now it has disappeared? I can't quite understand."

" I don't know how. The main thing is that it is now travelling about town in the disguise of a State Councillor. Therefore, I want to advertise, so that whoever catches it shall bring it to me in the shortest possible time. Judge for yourself! Really, how can I manage without such a conspicuous part of my body ? It is not as if it were the small toe on my foot which has disappeared, and which I could hide in high boots, and nobody would see whether it were there or not! On Thursdays I go to the State Councillor's wife, Chechtareva; Podtochina Pelageya Grivorievna, Staff Officer's wife—she has a very pretty daughter : they are very good friends of mine, and judge for yourself—what can I do ? I cannot appear there now! "

The official began to think, which was demonstrated by his firmly compressed lips.

" No! I cannot put such an advertisement in the paper," he said finally, after a long silence.

" Why ? Why not ? "

" For this reason—a newspaper may lose its reputation. If everybody began to write that his nose had run away from him, then . . . ! As it is, people say that many absurd and false rumours are being printed."

" But why is this matter absurd ? There is nothing absurd about it! "

" That is how you see it. But then last week a similar thing happened. An official came in, just as you came to-day, and brought a written notice. According to calculation, the cost amounted to 2 roubles 73, and all the advertisement consisted of was the fact that a black-haired poodle had run away. On the face of it, what is wrong

with that ?   But it resulted in a libel action.   That poodle
was a treasurer—I don't remember of what department."

"But I am not advertising for a poodle! I am advertising for my own nose—therefore, almost about
myself!"

"No! On no account can I take such an advertisement."

"But my nose has really disappeared!"

"If it has disappeared, it is a matter for a medical man.
They say that there are people who can give you any nose
you desire. But, by the way, I realise that you must be
a man with a gay nature and like to indulge in a joke
when in company."

"I swear to you! And, as things have gone so far, I'll
show you."

"Why take the trouble ?" replied the official, taking
snuff. "On the other hand, if it is not too much trouble,"
he added, with curiosity, "it would be interesting to have
a look at it."

The collegiate assessor removed the handkerchief from
his face.

"And so it is—very strange!" said the official. "The
place is quite smooth, like a freshly fried pancake. Yes,
yes, incredibly smooth!"

"Will you stop arguing now? You can see for yourself
that it is imposible not to print it! I shall be extremely
grateful to you, and I am very glad that this incident has
afforded me the pleasure of making your acquaintance."

You can see from this that the collegiate assessor had
by this time decided to ingratiate himself a little.

"Of course, it is a small matter to print it," said the
official, "but I cannot see any advantage in it for you.
If you want to do it, give it to somebody clever at writing,
to describe it as a rare work of nature, and print an article
about it in the 'Northern Bee'" (here he again took a
pinch of snuff) "for instruction" (here he wiped his nose),
"or generally for the sake of everybody's curiosity."

The collegiate assessor completely lost all hope. He let

his glance travel over the newspaper, where various theatre performances were advertised. He was almost prepared to smile on seeing the name of an actress, of pretty appearance, and his hand went into his pocket to see whether he had on him a blue banknote, as Staff Officers, in Kovalev's opinion, should sit in the stalls: but the thought of the nose spoilt it all.

The official himself was apparently touched by Kovalev's predicament. Wishing to lighten his sorrow somewhat, he thought it appropriate to show his sympathy in a few words. "It really grieves me very much that such a curious thing should have happened to you. Would you care for a pinch of snuff? That cures headaches and sorrowful moods: it is even good for hæmorrhoids." Saying this, the official offered Kovalev the snuff box, having very deftly turned up the lid bearing the portrait of some lady wearing a hat.

This unpremeditated action made Kovalev lose his patience. "I do not understand how you can find this a suitable time for joking," he said with feeling, "don't you see that I do not possess the very thing to sniff with? May the Devil take your snuff!" Having said this, he left the newspaper office, deeply upset, and departed to the Commissioner of Police.

Kovalev entered the Commissioner's office just when the latter had stretched himself and yawned and had said to himself, "Now I'll have a pleasant two hours' sleep," and, therefore, as may be supposed, the collegiate assessor's arrival was very badly timed. The Commissioner greatly encouraged art and industry, but he preferred Government banknotes to anything else. "This banknote," he used to say, "there is nothing better. It does not ask for food, takes up little space, will always go into the pocket and will not break if you drop it."

The Commissioner received Kovalev somewhat frigidly and said that after lunch was not the time to make investigations; that nature itself ordered some rest after a good meal (from this the collegiate assessor could gather that the sayings of the ancient sages were not unknown to the Commissioner); that a nose could not be torn away from a decent man. This touched Kovalev on the raw.

It is necessary to point out that Kovalev was very easily offended. He could forgive anything said about him in his personal capacity, but any reflection on his rank or profession was unpardonable. He acquiesced in the privilege of the stage to ridicule subalterns, but would countenance no reference to the Officers of the Staff. The Commissioner's reception embarrassed him so much that he shook his head and said, with dignity, slightly extending his hands, " I confess I can say nothing more after such insulting remarks ..." and left.

He arrived home, hardly able to drag one foot after the other. Dusk was falling. His flat seemed to him wretched and extremely odious after all these unsuccessful searches. Entering the hall, he saw his man-servant, Ivan, lying on his back on a dirty leather settee, spitting methodically at the ceiling, and quite successfully hitting the same spot every time. The man's indifference infuriated him : he struck him on the head with his hand, crying " Pig ! You are always doing something idiotic ! "

Ivan immediately jumped up and rushed to take off Kovalev's cloak.

The Major entered his room, weary and sad, threw himself on a chair and, finally, after several sighs, said, " My God ! My God ! Why have I deserved such misfortune ? If I were without a hand or a foot, it would be bearable; but without a nose, a citizen is no citizen : you might just as well take him and throw him out of the window ! If it had been cut off in battle or a duel, or if it had gone through some fault of my own ! But it has gone for no reason at all—voluntarily, without any cause. But no, it cannot be true," he added after some thought, " it is impossible for a nose to disappear—absolutely impossible ! I am probably either dreaming or raving. Perhaps, by some mistake, instead of water I drank the vodka with which I wipe my beard after shaving. Ivan, the fool, forgot to take it away, and I probably swallowed it."

To assure himself that he was not drunk, the Major pinched himself so hard that he screamed. This pain quite persuaded him that it was all very real. He quietly approached the mirror, first screwing up his eyes, hoping that his nose might have appeared in its proper place; but the next minute he jumped back, saying, " What a dreadful sight! "

It was certainly incongruous. If a button, silver spoon, watch or anything similar had disappeared . . . but, for a nose to disappear! And, in addition, in one's own flat! Major Kovalev, considering all the circumstances, conjectured, perhaps nearer the truth than ever before, that the person responsible was none other than the Staff Officer's wife, Podtochina, who wanted him to marry her daughter. He had liked to flirt with her, but had evaded the final issue. When the Staff Officer's wife told him plainly that she would like him to marry the girl, he had quietly withdrawn with compliments, saying that he was still young; that he had to serve for another five years, after which he would be exactly forty years old. No doubt the Staff Officer's wife had decided to ruin him out of revenge and had employed some sorceress to that end, as it was impossible to suppose that the nose had been cut off. Nobody had entered his room, and the barber, Ivan Yakovlevitch, had shaved him as recently as Wednesday; and during the whole of Wednesday, and even Thursday, his nose was all there—he remembered distinctly. In any case, he would have felt pain, and the wound could not have healed so quickly and become as smooth as a pancake. He thought out plans. Should he start formal legal proceedings against the Staff Officer's wife, or go to her himself and accuse her personally? His meditation was interrupted by the sight of a light gleaming through the chink of the door, indicating that the candle in the hall had already been lit by Ivan. Soon Ivan himself appeared, carrying it before him and illuminating the whole room. Kovalev's first movement was to snatch the handkerchief and cover that part of his face where, yesterday, his nose had been, to avoid his stupid servant's gaping at the curious sight which his master's face presented.

Ivan had hardly had time to reach his dirty palliasse when a strange voice was heard in the hall, saying, " Does the collegiate assessor Kovalev live here?"

" Come in. Major Kovalev is here," said Kovalev hurriedly, jumping up and opening the door.

A police official entered; a handsome man, with side whiskers not too light nor too dark, and plump-cheeked; the same who had stood at the end of the Isaaky Bridge at the beginning of the story.

" Have you lost your nose? "

" That's right."

" It has been found."

" What are you saying? " exclaimed Major Kovalev. Joy robbed him of speech. He gaped at the officer, who was standing in front of him and on whose full lips and cheeks the trembling light of the candle twinkled brightly.

" By a strange coincidence, it was intercepted almost on the road. It was already seated in the coach and intended to travel to Riga. Its passport had been issued a long time ago in the name of an official. The strange thing is that I, myself, had at first taken it for a gentleman, but, luckily, I had my glasses with me, and, when I put them on, I saw at once that it was a nose. I am short-sighted, and, if you stand up in front of me, I can only see that you have a fact, but cannot distinguish either nose or beard. My mother-in-law—that is my wife's mother—does not see anything either."

Kovalev was beside himself. " Where is it? Where? I shall rush to it immediately."

" Don't bother. Knowing that you needed it, I have brought it with me. Strangely enough, the chief ac-

complice in this matter is the scoundrel barber from the
Voznesiensky Street, who is at present sitting in a cell. I
have suspected him for a long time of drunkenness and
theft, and even two days ago he stole a card of buttons
from a shop. Your nose is as good as new." Thereupon,
the District Officer delved into his pocket and extracted
from it the nose, wrapped in a piece of paper.

"Yes, that's it!" exclaimed Kovalev. "That's it
all right! Have a cup of tea with me."

"I should deem it a great pleasure, but on no account
can I do so. I have to drive from here to the gaol . . . The
price of food has risen a lot . . . I have also my mother-in-
law—that is, my wife's mother—living with me, and
children: the eldest especially is promising; a very clever
youngster, but there are no means at all for education . . ."

For some minutes after the police officer's departure, the
collegiate assessor remained almost in a trance, and only
regained his senses after another few minutes. He was
overwhelmed by the intensity of this unexpected joy.
Then, cautiously, he took his restored nose in the palms
of his hands and studied it closely.

"It's it—it's it all right," Major Kovalev cried. "Here
is the little pimple on the left which appeared yesterday."
The Major nearly laughed aloud with joy.

But nothing is permanent in this world, and even joy,
after the first few minutes, becomes less vivid, its intensity waning until, finally, imperceptibly, it merges into
the ordinary state of mind, as a ripple in a pool, born of
the fall of a stone, merges finally with the smooth surface.
Kovalev began to meditate, and the realisation dawned
upon him that the matter was not yet settled: the nose
had been found, but it had still to be attached—to be put
back in its place.

"And what if it will not stick?" Having put this
question to himself, the Major became pale. Filled with
inexplicable dread, he dashed to the table and moved as
near as possible to the mirror, so as not to misplace the

nose. His hands were trembling. Carefully and warily, he put his nose in its former place. Oh, horror! The nose would not stick! He put it to his mouth, warmed it a little with his breath, and again moved it to the smooth space between his two cheeks; but nothing would make the nose stick.

"Come on, cling, you fool!" he cried to the nose; but the nose was as lifeless as a piece of wood, and kept falling on to the table and producing the sound of a falling cork. The Major's face twisted into a grimace. "It must stick!" he cried, frightened. But all his efforts were in vain.

He called Ivan and sent him for the doctor, who occupied the best flat on the second floor of the same house. The doctor was a handsome man and possessed beautiful, pitch-black side whiskers and a fresh, healthy wife. He ate fresh apples every morning, and kept his mouth unusually clean, washing it out every morning for almost three-quarters-of-an-hour, and polishing his teeth with five different kinds of tooth-brushes.

The doctor arrived almost at once. Having enquired when the misfortune had occurred, he lifted Major Kovalev by his chin and rapped with his thumb on the place where the nose used to be, so that the Major had to throw back his head with such force that he hit the wall with the back of his head. The medical man said that this was nothing to worry about, and, having advised the Major to move slightly from the wall, ordered him to bend his head to the right. Having felt the place where the nose used to be, he said "Ahem!" Then he ordered the Major to bend his head to the left, and said "Ahem!" Finally, he again rapped him with his thumb, so that Major Kovalev jerked his head like a horse whose teeth are being inspected. After this examination, the doctor shook his head and said, "No, impossible! You'd better stay as you are, or you may be worse off. Of course, it is possible to fix it; I could even fix it now; but I assure you that it would be worse for you."

"I like that! How can I remain without a nose?" said Kovalev. "It could not be worse than it is now. The Devil knows what I am to do! How can I show myself in this idiotic state? I have important acquaintances. . . . For example, to-day I am invited to receptions at two houses. I know many people, the State Councillor's wife, Chechtareva, the Staff Officer's wife Podtochina . . . after this occurrence I shall have nothing more to do with her, unless it be through the police. Please help me," continued Kovalev in an imploring tone, "isn't there some remedy? Fix it somehow, however badly, if it will only stay put. I could even support it slightly with my hand on dangerous occasions. And I don't dance, so that I can't harm it with some incautious movement. Any recompense for your visit, be assured, as far as my means will allow . . ."

"Believe it or not," said the doctor, neither loudly nor quietly, but extremely soothingly and convincingly, "I never visit for gain : it's against my convictions and my art. It is true that I charge for my visits, but merely in order not to hurt by refusal. I could, of course, fix your nose; but I can assure you, upon my honour, if you do not believe my word, that it would be the worse for you. Leave it to the work of nature herself. Wash the place frequently with cold water, and I assure you that, even without a nose, you will be as healthy as if you had one. As for the nose, I would advise you to put it in a jar with spirit, or, even better, with a mixture of two tablespoons of strong vodka and warmed vinegar, and then you may get a considerable sum for it. I will buy it myself if you won't overcharge."

"No, no! Nothing would induce me to sell it!" cried Major Kovalev in desperation, "I'd rather it perished!"

"What is there to be done? At least, you can see that I have tried." Having said this, the elegant doctor left the room.

Kovalev had not even noticed the doctor's face, and, in

his deep preoccupation, had only seen the cuffs of his white shirt, as clean as snow, which peeped out from the sleeves of his black frock-coat.

The next day he decided, before starting formal proceedings, to write to the Staff Officer's wife in order to find out whether she would, without a legal struggle, undo the wrong done to him. The letter was as follows:
"Dear Madam,

Alexandra Grigorievna,

I cannot understand the strange deed you have perpetrated.

I assure you that, by acting in this manner, you will gain nothing, and will never force me to marry your daughter.

Believe me, the story about my nose is well known, as is also the fact that you are the principal person responsible, and nobody else. Its sudden departure from its place, its flight and masquerade, first as an official, and finally as itself, has been caused only by sorcery, practised by you, or by those who, like you, engage in such dishonourable occupations. It is my duty to warn you that, if the above-mentioned nose does not return to its place in the course of to-day, I shall have no alternative but to seek the protection of the law.

I have the honour to be, incidentally with the deepest respect for you,
Your obedient servant,
PLATON KOVALEV."

"Dear Sir,

Platon Kuzmich,

I was extremely astonished by your letter. I confess frankly, I never expected it, especially the unwarranted rebuke it contains.

I must advise you that I never received the official whom you mention, either disguised or undisguised.

It is true that Philip Ivanovitch used to visit me. It is also true that he sought my daughter's hand, and, although he is a man of good and steady habits and very learned, I never offered him any hope.

You also refer to a nose. If, by this, you imply that I wanted to lead you by the nose and then give you a formal refusal, then you surprise me. As you yourself imply, I was, on the contrary, of an entirely different opinion and, even now, if you would seek my daughter in marriage in the proper way, I am prepared to accept you at once, as this has always been my greatest desire. Hoping which, I remain ever at your service.

ALEXANDRA PODTOCHINA."

" No ! " said Kovalev, having read the letter, " she really is not guilty. Impossible ! The letter is written in a way in which a person guilty of a crime could never write." The collegiate assessor was wise in such matters, as he had been several times detailed to attend inquests while he was still in the Caucasus.

" How on earth could it have happened? Only the Devil can know," he finally concluded, disheartened.

In the meantime, the news about this unusual occurrence—and, as usual, some additional details—had spread. It was at a time when everybody's thoughts had been directed to the supernatural. Only a short time before, the public had been engrossed with experiments in spiritualism. The story about the dancing chairs on Koniushenaya Street was still quite fresh, and so it was little wonder that people soon began to say that the collegiate assessor Kovalev's nose paraded on the Nevsky Prospect at precisely three o'clock. A crowd of curious people congregated there every day. Somebody said that the nose was inside the Junker Stores : and such a crowd collected near Junker's that even the police had to interfere. One opportunist of honourable appearance, with side-whiskers, who sold stale pastries at the theatre entrance, constructed some wonderful solid wooden benches especially for the purpose of inviting the curious to stand on them at the price of eighty kopeks a head. One very worthy colonel left his house early for that very reason, and, with great difficulty, threaded his way through the crowd; but, to his great indignation, he saw in the shop window, instead of the nose, an ordinary woollen vest and a lithographic picture depicting a girl straightening her stocking and a dandy, in a fancy waistcoat and with a small beard, looking at her from behind a tree—a picture which had been hanging in the same place for more than ten years. He moved away and said, with annoyance, "How can people mislead the crowd with such foolish and incredible rumours?" Then he said, loudly, that the Major's nose was promenading, not on the Nevsky Prospect, but in the Tavricheski Gardens; that apparently it had been there for some time; that, even, when Chozrev-Mirza used to live there, he was very much surprised at this strange trick of nature. Some of the students from the Surgical Academy departed there. One eminent and respectable lady asked the superintendent of the Gardens in a special letter to show her children this rare phenomenon and, if possible, to give an explanation which would instruct and edify youth.

All the indispensable social guests at balls and receptions, who like to make the ladies laugh and whose stock at this time was completely exhausted, were extremely pleased by these happenings. A small party of honourable and well intentioned people showed extreme displeasure. One gentleman said, with indignation, that he could not understand how, in the present enlightened age, such absurd stories could spread and that he was amazed that the Government had not done something about it. This gentleman apparently belonged to those who would entangle the Government in everything—even their daily squabbles with their wives.

After that . . . but here again the whole affair is obscured by mist, and what followed is unknown.

3

The world is full of absolute nonsense. Sometimes there is no way of understanding it. Suddenly the very

D

same nose, which had travelled about in the guise of a State Councillor and made such a noise in the town, found itself, as if nothing had happened, back in its place —that is, between Major Kovalev's two cheeks. This had already happened by the 7th day of April.

Having awoken, and automatically glanced in the mirror, Kovalev saw—the nose! He grasped it with his hand—yes, it was really his nose! "Well!" said Kovalev, and, barefoot as he was, nearly began to dance a trepak with joy. The entrance of Ivan restrained him. He immediately ordered a wash basin and towel, and, washing himself, looked again in the mirror—the nose was still there. Wiping himself with the towel, he again looked into the mirror—he still had a nose.

"Ivan, look here. I think I have a little pimple on my nose," he said, and thought, "How terrible if Ivan says, 'No, sir, there is not only no pimple there—there is no nose either.'" But Ivan said, "No, sir, there's no pimple. Your nose is clear."

"Dash it—that's good!" the Major said to himself, and snapped his fingers.

At that moment the barber, Ivan Yakovlevitch, peeped through the door, but timidly, like a cat which has just been beaten for stealing some fat.

"Tell me first—are your hands clean?" shouted Kovalev to him from the distance.

"Quite clean, your Honour."

"You liar!"

"I swear by the Almighty, sir, they are clean."

"Well, be careful."

Kovalev sat down. Ivan Yakovlevitch covered him with a serviette, and, in a moment, with the aid of a brush, transformed his beard and part of his cheek into a froth of snowy whiteness like that offered on merchant's birthdays.

"Am I dreaming?" Ivan Yakovlevitch said to himself, suddenly seeing the nose, and, bending his head, looked

at it from the other side. "Upon my soul, can it really
be?" he continued, and looked at the nose for a long
time. At last, gently and with the greatest care imagin-
able, he raised two fingers to take it by its tip, such being
Ivan Yakovlevitch's method.

"Go carefully!" shouted Kovalev.

Ivan Yakovlevitch lowered his hand. He became
panic-stricken and embarrassed, as he had never been
before. Finally, he began to scrape carefully with the
razor under Kovalev's chin and beard, and, although it
was awkward and difficult to shave without support from
that part of the body with which one smells, nevertheless,
managing to press his rough thumb against the Major's
cheek and lower jaw, he at last surmounted all obstacles
and finished the shaving.

When everything was ready, Kovalev hurriedly dressed
and immediately took a cab and drove to the café. As
soon as he entered, he shouted from afar, " Boy, a cup of
chocolate!" and immediately rushed to a mirror—the
nose was still there. He turned round gaily and looked
patronisingly, slightly closing his eyes, at two army men,
one of whom had a nose no larger than a waistcoat button.

He then left for the office of the department where
he had applied for a Vice-Governor's post, or, in case of
failure, an executive one. Passing through the reception
room, he glanced at the mirror—he still had a nose.

Then he drove to the house of another collegiate
assessor, or major—a great humorist. On his way
there he thought, " If even the Major refrains from bursting his sides with laughing on seeing me, then it will
be a sure sign that everything is in its right place."
The collegiate assessor did not, however, even bat an eye-
lid. "That's good, that's good dammit!" thought
Kovalev to himself.

Proceeding on his way, he met the Staff Officer's wife,
Podtochina, with her daughter. He bowed to them and
was greeted with joyous cries—apparently there was

nothing wrong with him. He talked to them for a long
time, and, taking out his snuff-box with deliberation,
slowly filling both nostrils with snuff, thinking, " Serves
you right, women hens! I still shan't marry the
daughter. All you can have is a flirtation.''

Thereafter Major Kovalev gallivanted, as if nothing
had happened, on the Nevsky Prospect, in the theatres
and everywhere. And the nose, too, as if nothing had
happened, sat on his face without the slightest hint that
it had ever strayed in various directions. And ever after
Major Kovalev was to be seen, eternally good humoured
and smiling and pursuing pretty women—even, on one
occasion, entering a shop on the market-place and buying
some official ribbon, although for reasons unknown, as
he himself was no Knight of any Order.

Such is the story of what happened in the Northern
Capital of our spacious State. Only now can we realise that,
taking everything into consideration, there is much in it
that is incredible. Apart from the supernatural departure
of the nose—strange as that was—and its appearance in various places in the shape of a State Councilllor,
why on earth did not Kovalev tumble to the fact that
it is impossible to advertise for a nose through a newspaper office? I do not mean this in the sense that I think
it too extravagant to pay for an advertisement—that
would be nonsense, and I am by no means one for misers
—but it is unseemly, awkward, bad. Again, how did
the nose happen to turn up in the baked bread, and how
could Ivan Yakovlevitch himself . . . ? No, I cannot
understand this at all—definitely not! But even
stranger and more incomprehensible is that authors should
choose such subjects. I will confess that it is entirely
inconceivable—that it is really . . . ! No, no! I do not
understand it at all. First of all, it is of absolutely no value
to the Fatherland; secondly . . . and secondly too, it is
of no use at all. I simply do not know what the . . .

Yet taking everything into account—although, of

course, one can assume one thing and another and a third
—perhaps even . . . Well yes—and yet, what happen-
ing is without some absurdity? When you come to think
of it, there is really something in all this. Whatever anybody may say, such things do happen in the world—
seldom, but they do happen.

MIKHAIL
SALTYKOV-SHCHEDRIN

THE IDEALS OF A CARP

THE Carp and the Ruffe could never agree. The
Carp considered that honesty was the best policy,
while the Ruffe maintained that a little cunning
went a long way. There is no telling what exactly the
Ruffe meant by cunning, but whenever he used this word
the Carp burst out indignantly: "Oh, how despicable!"
To this the Ruffe would reply: "Time will show which
of us is right!"

The carp is a docile fish with idealistic tendencies. It
is not for nothing that monks are so fond of it. It spends
most of its time on the river-bed, where things are very
peaceful, or at the bottom of a pond, buried in the slime,
feeding on minute shell-fish, and naturally from time to
time it gets ideas, and occasionally these are somewhat
advanced. However, since carp do not have to submit
their ideas to a censor, nor to register their address at a
police station, there is no one to suspect them of being
politically unreliable. If men do sometimes lie in wait
for them, it is not because carp are free-thinkers but because they taste good.

Usually carp are caught with nets, but to get a good
catch you must know how to set about it. Experienced
fishermen choose a time just after it has been raining,

when the water is troubled, and as they cast their nets they beat the water with ropes or sticks and make a noise generally. The carp, hearing these sounds and thinking that they herald the triumph of free-thought, come up to see whether they can take part in the celebrations. That is why so many of them get caught and fall victim to human gluttony; for, as I said before, the carp makes such a tasty dish (especially when fried in sour cream) that marshals of nobility are apt to have them served even when entertaining the governor of their district.

The ruffe on the other hand is tinged with scepticism and is a prickly fish. However, when used for making fish-soup, it produces a stock which has no equal.

I have no idea how the Carp and the Ruffe met in the first instance. I only know that having met they at once began to argue. They argued at their first meeting, and at their next, and then they grew to enjoy these arguments so much that they made appointments to meet. They would come together under some spreading water-weed and make highbrow conversation, which was most edifying for the roach playing about nearby.

It was always the Carp who opened the debate.

" I don't believe," he said, " that struggle and strife can be the normal condition for the development of all living beings. I believe in progress without bloodshed, I believe in harmony, and I am deeply convinced that happiness is not the empty fantasy of dreamers, but that sooner or later a day will come when it will be accessible to all."

" One can but wait!" said the Ruffe sarcastically.

His words were usually abrupt, because he could not keep calm in an argument. The Ruffe was a highly-strung fish which had apparently suffered much. His heart was full to overflowing. Yes, he had plenty on his mind. He was not actually embittered, but the days when he had been a trusting and unsophisticated fish were now a thing of the dim past. All around he found strife instead of

peace and well-being, and general barbarity instead of
progress. He maintained that everyone who hoped to
survive had to reckon with all this. He looked upon the
Carp as a simpleton, but at the same time felt that it was
to the Carp alone that he could talk of the things that lay
nearest to his heart.

"Not only shall I wait, but I shall actually see that day
dawn," replied the Carp; "and not I alone, but everybody. The darkness in which we swim is the result of
some deplorable historic accident; but we have reached
an age when scientific research can investigate historic
accidents, and once their causes are known a way will
be found to eliminate them. Our present darkness is an
established fact; light is a hope for the future; there must,
there will be light!"

"So you imagine a time will come when there will
be no more pike?"

"What pike?" asked the Carp in surprise; he was so unsophisticated that whenever he heard the proverb quoted,
that the pike had been created to teach carp vigilance, he
had thought that this referred to some make-believe monster invented to frighten little children; naturally therefore he was not a bit afraid himself.

"Oh, you simpleton, you simpleton! Here you are
ready to solve world problems, and you have no idea what
a pike is."

The Ruffe flapped his fins in scorn and swam away,
but a little later the two met again in some secluded
spot—it can be very boring in the water—and the
discussion began all over again.

"Good is the most important thing in life," the Carp
would hold forth, carried away by his own eloquence.
"It is just owing to a misunderstanding that evil has
crept in, for the vital force of life dwells in good."

"Open your mouth and shut your eyes."

"Oh, Ruffe, what inappropriate expressions you use!
Is that a suitable answer to my argument?"

"You don't deserve any answer at all. You are just stupid, that's what you are."

"Now Ruffe, do listen to what I am saying. History will bear me out that evil has never been a constructive force. Evil crushed, suppressed, pillaged and laid waste by sword and fire, but good was always a constructive force. It rushed to the aid of the oppressed and freed them from bondage; it stirred minds and aroused sentiments which bear good fruit. Had there not been this truly constructive factor in life, there would have been no history. For after all, what is history? History is the saga of liberation, it is the story of the triumph of good and reason over evil and madness."

"And, of course, you know for certain that evil and madness have been put to shame?" mocked the Ruffe.

"They have not been put to shame yet, but they will be, you mark my words. Again I will refer you to history. Just compare what existed in bygone days with what we have now, and you will be forced to agree that not only the outward expression of evil has been modified but that the sum total of evil has decreased perceptibly. Just take us fishes for example. Once we could be caught at any time, and particularly in the breeding season, when we lose our heads and make straight for fishermen's nets of our own accord. Whereas now it's considered harmful to catch us during the breeding season. Formerly we were destroyed by quite barbarous methods: they say that in the Ural river, for instance, when harpooning was allowed, the water would be dyed red for miles with our blood; but all that is at an end now. Fishing-rods and nets and nothing else may be used. Even so, there are special committees to decide whether nets may or may not be used in this or that particular case."

"So apparently it is not just the same to you by what means you land finally in fish-soup?"

"What is fish-soup?" asked the Carp in surprise.

"Oh, good heavens! You call yourself a Carp and have never heard of fish-soup! What right have you to talk after that? Those who take part in discussions and hope to defend their views, should first of all have some idea of their facts. How can you hold forth if you don't know the simple truth that carp eventually end up in fish-soup. Get out before I impale you on one of my spines."

The Ruffe looked so fierce with his spines standing up that the Carp sank down to the bottom as quickly as his own clumsiness would allow. But some twenty-four hours later the two friendly antagonists had met again and opened a new debate.

"A pike visited our creek to-day," announced the Ruffe.

"Is that the pike you mentioned the other day?"

"Yes. It swam in, had a look round and said: 'This looks far too peaceful, there must be carp here,' and swam away."

"What am I to do now?"

"Oh, you just prepare yourself, that's all. When the pike arrives and sets its huge eyes on you, just hug your fins and scales closer together, and then down the pike's gullet you go."

"Why on earth should I? I haven't done anything wrong."

"You're a fool, that's what's wrong with you. For another thing you're plump. There is a law which says that the right place for fat and stupid carp is down a pike's gullet."

"There can't possibly be such a law," said the Carp with sincere indignation." "Besides, the pike has no right to swallow anyone without first demanding an explanation. I'll explain everything to it quite truthfully. Once it has heard the truth, all will be well."

"I told you you were a simpleton. How many more times must I repeat the same thing: simpleton, simpleton,

simpleton!"

The Ruffe was quite cross this time and swore that in future he would have nothing more to do with the Carp. A few days later, however, the old habit had triumphed.

"If only fishes would come to an agreement." began the Carp with a far-away look in his eyes.

This time the Ruffe himself was apprehensive. "What on earth is the Carp leading up to?" he thought. "Any moment he may come out with something quite unsuitable, and there's a chub swimming about here. Just look at the cunning fellow pretending to look the other way, as though we were no concern of his, and, I bet, listening for all he's worth."

"There's no need to utter every word that comes into your mind," he said, trying to warn the Carp; "nor to open your mouth as wide as it will go. There's such a thing as whispering, you know."

"I don't want to talk in a whisper," bellowed the Carp unperturbed. "What I have to say I say quite openly, and that is, that if all fishes would agree, then . . ."

Here the Ruffe rudely interrupted his friend.

"It's no good talking to you," he shouted, and swam away as quickly as his fins would carry him.

He was both annoyed and sorry for the Carp who, notwithstanding his foolishness, was really the only fish with whom you could have a heart-to-heart talk. He would never repeat what you had said or betray you in any way, and where are such qualities to be found now-a-days, when such bad times are upon us that one cannot rely even on one's own father or mother? Of course, there is nothing downright bad about the roach, but you never know where you are with them: some day they may blab quite unwittingly. But when it comes to the chub, tench and other riff-raff, well! Offer them a worm, and they are ready to testify under oath to anything. Poor old Carp is quite wasted among this lot.

"Just you take a look at yourself," he said to the Carp. "What sort of defence can you put up in an hour of need? Your body is large, your head is too small to think up anything and your mouth tiny. Even your scales are not up to much. You have no cunning and no agility, you clumsy old thing. There's just nothing to stop anyone who feels like it from swimming up to you and eating you."

"But why should anyone eat me, when I haven't done any harm?" persisted the Carp.

"Listen, you chump. Do you really imagine that one gets eaten because one has done something? You don't get eaten because you deserve to be executed, but because someone is hungry; that's all there is to it. Incidentally you yourself eat, don't you? It's not for nothing that you stick your nose into the slime and rummage about for shell-fish. They want to live, but you, simpleton, just fill yourself up with them from morning till night. What wrong have they done you that you are carrying out executions every other minute? You remember how you were saying a little while ago: 'If only all fishes would agree'? What if molluscs were included in this agreement, you half-wit? You'd be in a pretty tight corner yourself then, wouldn't you?"

The question was so direct and unpleasant that the Carp was confused and even blushed slightly.

"But molluscs after all are . . ." he muttered, perturbed.

"Molluscs are molluscs, and carp are carp. Carp enjoy molluscs, and pike enjoy carp. Neither the molluscs nor the carp have done wrong, yet they must both put up with their fate. You can ponder over this for a hundred years if you like, but you won't be able to change anything."

After this conversation the Carp hid himself deep in

the slime and began to think at his leisure. He thought
and thought and incidentally went on eating mollusc
after mollusc. The more he ate the more he felt like
eating. However, at last he arrived at some conclusions.

"I don't eat these molluscs because they have done
wrong, you're quite right there," he explained to the
Ruffe, "but I eat them because that is the food Nature
has provided for me."

"Whoever told you that?"

"No one has told me. This is based on my personal
observations. Molluscs have no soul, but just a kind of
vapour. When they are eaten they don't understand anything. Besides, they are created in such a way that it's
impossible to avoid swallowing them. All you have to
do is to take a gulp of water, and before you know where
you are, your mouth is full of these tiny things. I don't
really catch them, they just seem to float into my mouth.
Now a carp is an entirely different proposition: don't
forget, old man, that a carp can be eighteen inches long.
You must take a great deal into consideration before
eating someone of that size. Now if he had done something really wrong, that, of course, is quite another
matter."

"When a pike swallows you, you will see what crimes
justify being eaten. Until then it would be a good idea
if you just didn't talk so much."

"No, I shan't be silent. Even though I have never
seen a pike in my life and can only judge from what I
have heard, I know that they too cannot be deaf to the
voice of truth. Now tell me, do you really imagine such
a crime possible: here's a carp lying in the water, doing
no harm to anyone, and suddenly for no reason whatso-
ever he finds himself in a pike's stomach? I just can't
believe it."

"You extraordinary fellow! Why, the other day a
monk drew up two nets full of carp before your very
eyes. Do you think he's going to feast his eyes on

them?"

"I don't know, but then who can tell what has really happened to those carp? Maybe they are eaten, but perhaps they have been put into a fish-pool and are living there most happily at the expense of the monastery."

"Oh well, then you too had better go on living happily, you nit-wit."

Days passed, and there seemed to be no end to the discussions between the Carp and the Ruffe. The spot where they lived was very quiet with a lot of green slime floating on the surface of the water—an ideal spot for discussions. Under such circumstances you can say what you like and think what you choose with complete impunity. This so encouraged the Carp that he soared higher and higher into the realms of the ideal.

"Fishes should love each other," he held forth. "One for all and all for one. That is how true harmony will be attained."

"I should very much like to see you lavishing love on a pike."

"Oh, I shall know how to set about it," persisted the Carp. "I know some words which will instantaneously turn a pike into a carp."

"Out with them!"

"Oh, it's very simple. I shall just say to the pike: 'Do you know what virtue is, and what responsibilities towards our neighbours it entails?'"

"How wonderful! You wouldn't like me to spike you right through in reply to your question?"

"Oh, please don't joke about such things."

On another occasion the conversation ran thus:

"We fishes will only be conscious of our rights when we are taught from our earliest days to have a correct approach to citizenship."

"What on earth do you need it for?"

"Well, after all. . . ."

"After all!" mimicked the Ruffe. "A correct

approach to citizenship is of use only when there is scope for it. What are you going to do with it, lying in the slime?"

"I didn't mean in the slime, but generally speaking. . . ."

"For instance?"

"For instance, let's say a monk wants to cook me, then I would say to him: 'Brother, you have no right to inflict such a dreadful punishment on me without a trial.'"

"And he will throw you into a hot frying-pan or on to the fire for your insolence. No, you blockhead, what you need for living in slime is not a correct approach to citizenship, but an unreflecting one to all things. Then you just bury yourself where the slime is thickest and keep quiet."

"Fish should not feed on fish," raved the Carp on another occasion. "Nature has provided quite a lot of other delicious foods: molluscs, flies, worms, spiders, water-fleas, to say nothing of crayfish, frogs and snakes. All these are good and very suitable."

"And to the pike, carp seem very suitable," said the Ruffe, trying to sober the Carp down.

"Oh no, that argument is no good. If Nature has not provided us with weapons of defence such as you, Ruffe, have, for instance, this means that a special law ought to be published to protect us Carp."

"And if no one obeys that law?"

"Then an appeal should be issued, explaining that it's better not pass any laws at all if they are not carried out."

"And you think that would work?"

"I believe that many would be conscience-stricken."

Days sped by and the Carp babbled on. Another would have been brought to his senses in some way, but not he! What's more, he could have gone on with his harangues for years had he at least been careful. But he got carried away. On and on he talked, till all of a sudden the Chub served a notice on him, to the effect that the Pike would be visiting the creek on the following day and would he, Carp, appear before him at daybreak?

The Carp, however, was not frightened. Firstly, he had heard so many different accounts about the Pike that he wished to meet him personally, and secondly, he believed he possessed magic words which, if spoken even to the fiercest of pike, would transform it immediately into a carp. He had great faith in these words.

Seeing this great faith of his, even the Ruffe had some misgivings and began to think that perhaps he was wrong somewhere. What if it really were true that the Pike was only waiting for someone to love him and give him good counsel so that both his heart and mind could be flooded with a new light? What if the Pike were really kind? Then the Carp was not such a simpleton as would appear at first glance, but was in reality carving quite a fine career for himself. The following day he would appear before the Pike undaunted and come out with the whole truth, such as the Pike had never yet heard in all his born days. Then the Pike would say: "Carp, because you've spoken the truth, I grant you this creek, and you shall rule over it!"

Next morning, sure as life, the Pike appeared. The Carp looked at him in astonishment: to think of all the stories he had heard about him, and here he was—a fish, just like any other other fish; that is, except for the mouth, which reached from ear to ear, and the gullet, which was big enough to admit the Carp.

"I have heard," said the Pike, "that you, Carp, are a very able fellow and an eloquent speaker. I should like to have a little debate with you. Kindly open the discussion."

"Happiness is what I think about a great deal," said the Carp modestly, but with great dignity. "Not happiness for myself, but happiness for all. Every fish ought to swim about freely in all waters, and if any of them feel like hiding in the slime, well then, let them lie there undisturbed."

"I see. You believe such a state of affairs possible?"

"Not only do I believe this, but I am expecting it hourly."

"Do you mean that I, and, shall we say, a carp, should swim in the water side by side?"

"Yes, why not?"

"This is the first time I have heard of such a thing. What if I turn round and eat the carp?"

"There is no law according to which you could do such a thing, your Excellency. No, the law states very simply: molluscs, mosquitoes, flies and midges shall form the staple food of fishes. Then by various subsequent amendments the following have also been added to the list of permissible foods: water-fleas, beetles, spiders, worms, frogs, crayfish and other aquatic denizens. But not fish."

"That wouldn't suit me. Is there really such a law, Chub?" said the Pike turning to the Chub.

"I don't remember, Your Excellency," replied the Chub, cleverly extricating himself from a difficult situation.

"I knew there couldn't be such a law. Well, Carp, is there anything else you are expecting hourly?"

"Yes, Your Excellency: the triumph of Justice, when the strong can no longer oppress the weak and the rich the poor. Then I believe there will be a common cause in which every fish will play its part. You, Pike, because you are stronger and cleverer, will have a task to match your abilities, and to me, because my abilities are modest, a modest task will be allotted. Each of us for all, and all for each of us, that's how it will be. When we all stand up for each other no one can hurt us. If a fishing-net should appear, we shall all take to our fins and hide under stones, and roots, in the mud at the bottom, and in holes in the bank. Fish-soup will have to be abolished."

"I don't know so much about that. People are not too keen to give up things that taste good to them. And who knows when such things can come about, if ever? But here's an interesting point: according to your plan would I, too, be expected to do some work?"

"Naturally, like everybody else."

"I have never heard of such a thing. You'd better go and sleep it off.'"

Whether the Carp slept it off or not, there is no telling, but anyway he grew no wiser. At mid-day he returned and continued the discussion, not only undaunted, but more cheerful than ever.

"So you imagine that I ought to work while you enjoy the fruits of my labour?" asked the Pike straight out.

"Of each other's labour, of mutual labour for a common cause. . . ."

"Of each other's labour and incidentally mine! Hm! There's something fishy to me about all this. Chub, what is the correct term for such talk?"

"Sho-shillism, Your Excellency."

"I thought as much. For some time I have heard that the Carp was making seditious speeches, only I decided I had better first make sure personally. So that's what you're up to!"

Saying this the Pike splashed the water with his tail so eloquently that, for all his simplicity, the Carp guessed what was up.

"I, your Excellency," he mumbled, "I was simply . . ."

"That'll do. They say simplicity is worse than duplicity. If you let fools have their own way they'll make life impossible for the intelligent. I've heard reams and reams about you, but Carp, you are just a Carp and nothing more. I have spent barely five minutes with you, and I am bored to death."

The Pike was lost in thought, but he cast such a meaning glance at the Carp that the latter understood everything. However, apparently the Pike had been feasting
the day before, and was not yet hungry, for he gave a
yawn, which was followed immediately by snores.

But for all that the Carp's luck had deserted him. As
soon as the Pike stopped speaking, the Carp was surrounded by several chub who stood guard over him.

Later on in the afternoon, as the sun was setting, the
Carp appeared before the Pike for the third time. This
time he was brought in by an escort and did not look
his usual self, because while interrogating him Perch
had bitten off part of his tail and bits from his back.

He was, however, keeping a stiff upper lip, since he
still had his magic word in reserve.

"Although you hold views I do not share," began the
Pike, "I unfortunately simply adore discussions. So
carry on!"

At this the Carp felt his heart glowing within him.
He tensed his body, he quivered, splashed the water with
the remains of his tail and, looking the Pike straight in
the face, shouted at the top of his voice: "Do you know
what virtue is?"

The Pike opened his mouth in astonishment. He also
gulped in amazement and involuntarily happened to
swallow the Carp.

The fishes who witnessed the incident were dumb-
founded, but only for a moment. They came to their
senses immediately and rushed up to the Pike, to find
out whether His Excellency had partaken of his supper
satisfactorily and to make sure that His Excellency had
not choked. The Ruffe, who had foreseen and foretold
all this, swam well to the fore and announced with due
solemnity:

"That's the kind of discussion we have here!"

FYODOR DOSTOEVSKY

THE CROCODILE

AN UNUSUAL OCCURRENCE or EPISODE IN THE ARCADE

Being the true story of how a gentleman of middle age and middling appearance was swallowed alive, in toto, by a crocodile in the Arcade, and what came of it.

Ohé Lambert! Où est Lambert?
As-tu vu Lambert?

ON January the thirteenth of the present year, 1865, at half-past noon, Elena Ivanovna, wife of my cultured friend, colleague and to some extent distant relative Ivan Matveyich, expressed a desire to go and have a look at the crocodile on show for a small fee in the Arcade. Having in his pocket (not so much because of ill-health as out of curiosity pure and simple) his ticket for a trip to foreign parts, hence already being reckoned on leave of absence and thus quite free that morning, Ivan Matveyich not only raised no objection to his wife's frivolous desire but even seemed quite interested himself. " A marvellous idea!" he said, very contentedly. "Let's go and have a look at the crocodile. We are going to Europe, so while we're still here why not familiarize ourselves with the fauna of those parts? " And with these words, taking his wife by the arm, he at once set out with her for the Arcade. I, as usual, marched off at their side—for I am by the way of being a friend of the family. Never had I seen Ivan Matveyich more agreeably disposed than on that memorable morning; how true it is that we know not what fate has in store! Entering the Arcade, he at once began to expatiate on the magnificence of the architecture, and as we drew near to the shop housing the imported monster he himself offered to pay the crocodile-keeper my entrance-fee of twenty-five copecks. Such a thing had never happened before. On entering the small room we observed that in addition to the crocodile it contained parrots of the foreign or cacadou variety, and moreover a group of monkeys in a special cupboard in a recess. Right by the entrance, on the left, stood a large metal box rather like a bath-tub, covered with a thick iron netting, and with an inch or so of water at the bottom. In this shallow pool an enormous crocodile lay like a log, quite motionless, and apparently deprived of all its faculties by our damp and inhospitable climate. At first this monster roused no particular curiosity in any of us.

"So tha-at's the cwocodile!" said Elena Ivanovna in a sing-song, disillusioned voice. "I expected it to be . . . qu-i-ite diffewent!"

In all probability she had expected it to be made of diamonds. A German, the owner and exhibitor of the crocodile, came out to meet us, and looked at us in an extremely haughty manner.

"He's quite right," Ivan Matveyich whispered to me. "He knows that for the moment he's the sole crocodile-exhibitor in the whole of Russia."

I must attribute this absolutely frivolous remark to the exceptionally benevolent mood which had come over Ivan Matveyich, who was normally of quite an envious disposition.

"I don't believe it's alive," said Elena Ivanovna, piqued by the man's unbending demeanour; and with a gracious smile she turned to the surly fellow, aiming to win him over—a manoeuvre so characteristic of women.

"Oh yez id iss," retorted the man in his broken Russian, and half-raising the iron netting he began to poke the crocodile's head with a stick.

Then the cunning beast, to demonstrate that it was sentient, slightly twiddled its paws and its tail, and raising its snout emitted something in the nature of a prolonged snort.

"Don't be angry, Karlchen," said the German affectionately, his amour propre titillated.

"How beastly it is! Makes me feel quite funny!" lisped Elena Ivanovna still more coquettishly. "I am sure I shall see it in my dweams."

"But he von't bite you in your dreams," retorted the German with shopkeeper gallantry, and laughed before anyone else at his witty remark. But none of us responded.

"Come on, Semyon Semyonych," said Elena Ivanovna, addressing herself exclusively to me. "Let's go and look at the dear little monkeys. I'm so fond of monkeys; some of them are such absolute little darlings. As for the cwocodile, I think he's simply howwid."

"Don't be afraid, my love," Ivan Matveyich called after us, pleased at the idea of playing the hero before his wife. "This torpid denizen of Pharaoh's kingdom can't do a thing to us." And he remained behind. Indeed, taking his glove, he began to tickle the crocodile's nose with it, wishing, as he subsequently admitted, to make it snort again. As for the crocodile's owner, he followed the lady and myself to the monkey-cupboard.

So everything was lovely, and nothing could be foreseen. Elena Ivanovna was charmed to the point of sprightliness by the monkeys, and seemed to find them absolutely fascinating. She kept giving little cries of pleasure, turning to me, ostentatiously paying no attention to the German, and giggling at the similarity she observed between the monkeys and her intimate friends and acquaintances. I too felt quite tickled, for the likeness was undeniable. The proprietor didn't know whether to laugh or not, and so in the end grew quite sombre. And just at that moment a terrible—I might even say unnatural—cry shook the room. Quite at a loss, I first of all froze in my tracks; but realizing that Elena Ivanovna was also screaming I quickly turned round and—what did I see? I saw—merciful Heavens! —I saw the unhappy Ivan Matveyich in the terrible jaws of the crocodile, seized by them across the trunk, raised horizontally in the air and desperately kicking his legs. The next moment he was gone. But I will describe in detail what happened, for all the time I was standing there motionless, and able to follow the whole of the process taking place before me with an attention and curiosity I shall never forget. " For," I said to myself at that fatal moment, " supposing that had happened to me instead of Ivan Matveyich, how unpleasant it would have been!" But to return to my narrative. The crocodile commenced by turning poor Ivan Matveyich in its jaws legs first, and swallowing the legs; then, slightly regurgitating Ivan Matveyich, who, trying to extricate himself, was clinging to the edge of the box, it ingurgitated him once more, this time up to the waist. Then, after a slight secondary regurgitation, it gave one gulp, and then another. In this fashion Ivan Matveyich slowly vanished before our eyes. At length, with a final gulp, the crocodile absorbed the whole of my cultured friend, this time for good. On the crocodile's exterior could be read the way in which Ivan Matveyich's angular form was passing into its interior. I was on the point of crying out once more when fate chose to play another scurvy trick on us: the crocodile seemed to strain, no doubt choked by the enormity of the object it had swallowed, and once more opened its terrible maw; and from it, by way of a final regurgitation, there emerged for a moment the head of Ivan Matveyich, with a horrified expression on his face, and his glasses slipped from his nose and fell on the bottom of the box. It seemed as though this despairing head had emerged simply in order to cast a last glance at everything, and to bid a mute good-bye to all the pleasures of the world. But it was given no opportunity to do so; the crocodile gathered its forces, gulped, and in the twinkling of an eye the head had vanished—and this time for ever. This appearance and disappearance of a live human head was terrible, but at the same time—whether from the speed or the un-

expectedness of the occurrence, or because of the way
in which the glasses had fallen from the nose—
there was in it so comical an element that suddenly and
quite unexpectedly I gave a snort of amusement. The
next moment I realised how ill it became me, as a
friend of the family, to laugh; at once I turned to Elena
Ivanovna with a sympathetic expression, and said:

"Ivan Matveyich has shuffled off this mortal coil."

I cannot even think of trying to express how great had
been the agitation of Elena Ivanovna during the course
of the process I have described. First of all, after her
initial cry, she had seemed as though petrified, watching
the tragedy being enacted before her with apparent indifference but with extremely bulging eyes; then she
burst into a heart-breaking wail. I seized her by the
hands. At this moment the proprietor, who at first had
also been frozen with horror, suddenly clasped his hands
and cried, looking wildly upwards:

"Oh, my grogodile, *o mein allerliebster Karlchen!*
Mutter, Mutter, Mutter!"

At this cry the door at the rear opened and Mutter
came in, in a lace cap, red-cheeked and elderly, but
tousled, and with a shriek sprang towards her son.

Now Sodom and Gomorrha began: Elena Ivanovna
did nothing but cry hysterically "Whip him up!", leap-
ing around the proprietor and his Mutter, apparently
beseeching them—no doubt beside herself—to whip
someone up for some reason or other. But the proprietor and his Mutter paid no attention to any of us;
standing by the crocodile-box, the two of them were
mooing like a pair of calves.

"He'll die, he'll burst, for he's swallowed a whole
Government official!" cried the proprietor.

"*Unser Karlchen, unser allerliebster Karlchen wird
sterben!*" wailed his Mutter.

"We are orphans, without a grust to our names!"
went on the proprietor.

"Whip him up, whip him up, whip him up!" clamoured Elena Ivanovna, clutching the German's sleeve.

"He was deasing the grogodile; why was your man deasing the grogodile?" cried the German, shaking her off. "You'll have to bay, if *unser Karlchen* goes *platz. Das war mein Sohn, das war mein einziger Sohn!*"

I must confess I felt quite nettled at this display of selfishness on the part of a visiting German and hardness of heart by his tousled Mutter; nevertheless, Elena Ivanovna's reiterated cries of "Whip him up" roused my disquiet even more, and finally attracted the whole of my attention, so that I began to feel quite nervous. . . . I will anticipate by saying that this strange cry had been quite erroneously interpreted by me; I fancied that Elena Ivanovna must have gone off her head, but nevertheless, wishing to avenge the loss of her beloved Ivan Matveyich, was proposing, in order to slake her thirst for vengeance, that the crocodile should be scourged. But in fact she meant something quite different. Looking round at the door in no little confusion, I began to beg her to calm herself, and above all not to employ the somewhat sadistic word "whip." For so reactionary a desire, here, in the very heart of the Arcade, with all its cultured visitors, only two steps from the very hall in which, perhaps, at that very moment Mr. Lavrov was giving a public lecture, was not merely impossible, but even unthinkable, and at any moment might draw upon our heads the angry hisses of the cultured and the caricatures of Mr. Stepanov. To my horror I immediately proved right in my anxious forebodings; suddenly the curtain separating the crocodile-room from the little cubby-hole in which the entrance-fees were collected was drawn aside, and on the threshold appeared a figure with a beard and moustaches and holding a peaked cap in its hand. Bending the upper part of his body forward at an acute angle, the newcomer endeavoured very cautiously to keep his legs outside the crocodile-room, so as to be under no obligation to pay the entrance-fee.

"So retrograde a desire, madame," said the unknown semi-visitor, doing his best to remain outside the threshold and not topple over towards us, "does no honour to your mental development, and is conditioned by a lack of phosphorus in the brain. You will be held up to ridicule in the chronicle of progress, and in our satirical journals. . . ."

He could say no more; the proprietor, recovering his presence of mind, and perceiving a person talking in the crocodilery without having paid the entrance-fee, rushed furiously at the unknown progressive and, using both his fists, vigorously discharged him from the room. For a minute both were concealed from our eyes by the curtain, and it was only then that I realized that the whole disturbance had been over the merest trifle. Elena Ivanovna was not in the slightest degree to blame. She had had no idea, as I had previously imagined, of subjecting the crocodile to the reactionary and humiliating punishment of whipping. She had simply desired to have him ripped up with a knife, so that Ivan Matveyich might be liberated from his interior.

"Vot? You vant mine grogodile to berish?" wailed the proprietor, who had run in again. "Your man shall berish before mine grogodile does! Mine father exhibited the grogodile, mine son vill exhibit the grogodile. All vill exhibit the grogodile. I am known to *ganz Europa*, but you are not known to *ganz Europa*, and vill have to bay me a fine."

"*Ja, ja,*" caught up his infuriated Mutter. "We von't let you go; you shall bay a fine if Karlchen goes *platz!*"

"In any case," I added calmly, anxious to get Elena Ivanovna home without delay, "there is no point in ripping the crocodile open, since our dear Ivan Matveyich is no doubt by this time soaring in the empyrean."

"My friend," resounded at this moment, suddenly and quite unexpectedly, the voice of Ivan Matveyich, startling us extremely, "my friend, in my opinion the thing to do is to apply directly to the Public Prosecutor, for without the help of the police this Teuton will never see the light."

These words, enunciated firmly and weightily, and expressive of an unusual presence of mind, at first so startled us that we refused to believe our ears. But we ran up to the cocodile-box at once, and listened with as much awe as incredulity to the words of the unfortunate captive. His voice was thin and faint, as though proceeding from a considerable distance. It was rather like when the funny man of the party, going into the next room and covering his mouth with a pillow, begins to shout, demonstrating to the people in the other room what it sounds like when two peasants call to one another across a plain, or when separated by a deep ravine—a performance I had the pleasure of hearing once at a Christmas party given by some friends.

"Ivan Matveyich, my darling, so you're still alive!" lisped Elena Ivanovna.

"Alive and well," replied Ivan Matveyich; "thanks to Providence I was swallowed without suffering any lesions. All that worries me is how my superiors will view this occurrence; for, having received a ticket for foreign parts, I've gone and landed up inside a crocodile, which is not even witty."

"Don't wowwy about wit, my dear; the first thing we must do is somehow or other extwicate you," interrupted Elena Ivanovna.

"Don't you dare douch my grogodile!" cried the proprietor. "I von't allow my grogodile to be interfered with. Now mooch beoples vill gum to see him, and I shall be able to charge them *fünfzig* gopecks, and Karlchen vill be vell provided for."

"*Gott sei Dank!*" added his Mutter.

"They are quite right," observed Ivan Matveyich calmly. "The laws of economics must be respected before all else."

"My friend," I cried. "I'll dash off to your superiors this moment and lay a complaint, for I can see that by ourselves we shall never be able to cope with the matter."

"I am inclined to agree with you," said Ivan Matveyich. "But in our era of trade crises it is difficult to envisage ripping open the belly of a crocodile without rendering the owner some suitable compensation. So the first question that arises is: Who will furnish the required sum? For you are well aware of my financial position. . . ."

"Perhaps it might take the form of an advance on your salary," I suggested timidly, but the proprietor at once broke in:

"I vill not sell mine grogodile; not for three thousand vill I sell him, not for four thousand! Now mooch beoples vill gum. Not for five thousand vill I sell him."

In a word, he made an absolute nuisance of himself; his eyes gleamed with base covetousness.

"I'll go this moment!" I cried, indignant.

"And so will I!" piped Elena Ivanovna. "I'll go and see Andrey Osipych straight away, and soften his heart with my tears."

"Don't do that, my dear," Ivan Matveyich hurried to interrupt; he had long been jealous of Andrey Osipych, and he knew that she would love to hurry off and shed tears before a cultured man, for tears suited her tremendously. "Nor do I advise you to, my friend," he went on to me; "you mustn't dash straight off to the authorities like that; heaven knows what the outcome would be. It would be much better if you were to drop in to-day on Timofey Semyonych, by way of a private call; he's a rather old-fashioned chap, and not too bright, but he's dependable, and above all as straight as a die. Give him my respects, and explain the circumstances in which I find myself. And as I owe him the sum of seven roubles from our last game of whist, you might take the opportunity to let him have it; it will touch the stern old man. In any case his advice may serve to guide us. And now take Elena away for the time being. . . . Calm yourself, my dear," he went on to her; "all this shrieking and female nonsense has wearied me, and I should like to take a proper look at the cosy corner in which I so unexpectedly find myself. . . ."

"Take a pwoper look . . . ? D'you mean you have a light in there?" cried Elena Ivanovna, overjoyed.

"I am wrapped in impenetrable night," replied the poor captive; "but I can grope about, and as it were take a look with my hands. Good-bye for the present, then; don't worry, and don't allow this to disturb your mind. Till tomorrow. But I'd like you, Semyon Semyonych, to look in this evening; as you're rather forgetful, perhaps you might tie a knot in your handkerchief. . . ."

I must confess that I was glad to get away; I was feeling very tired, and even a bit bored. Giving my arm to Elena Ivanovna, who, though grieving, had been rendered even prettier by her agitation, I hasten to conduct her from the crocodilery.

"You'll have to pay another twenty-five gopecks if you gum this evening!" the proprietor called after us.

"Goodness, how avid they are!" said Elena Ivanovna, looking into every mirror as we passed along the Arcade, and obviously aware of the fact that she was looking prettier than ever.

"The laws of economics," I replied, rather excited, and pleased to be seen in public with so delightful a companion.

"The laws of economics . . ." she said in her charming drawl. "I didn't understand a word that Ivan Matveyich was saying about them just now."

"I will explain," I said, and at once commenced to expound the beneficent results of attracting foreign capital to our country; I had been reading about it that morning in the papers.

"How queer!" she interrupted. when she had listened to me for a while. "And now please stop explaining; it sounds absolute nonsense to me. But tell me : is my face vewwy wed?"

"Not wed but wavishing," I said, seizing the opportunity to pay her a compliment.

"You naughty man!" she lisped, well pleased. "Poor Ivan Matveyich!" she added a minute later, bending her head coquettishly to one side. "I weally feel quite sowwy for him.—My goodness!" she suddenly exclaimed. "How on earth will he manage about having his meals and . . . and evewything?"

"That's a point that hadn't occurred to me," I said, also taken aback. This aspect of the affair had never entered my head, which just goes to show how much more practical women are in dealing with the problems of life.

"The poor dear, when you think of him tucked away in there . . . and with nothing to do . . . and in the dark. . . . What a pity I haven't a single photograph of him!—So now I suppose I'm a sort of widow," she added with a fascinating smile, obviously intrigued by her new condition. "Still . . . I weally am sowwy for him!"

In a word, she expressed the quite understandable and natural grief of a young and attractive wife for a departed husband. At last I got her home and calmed her down, and after having dinner with her and taking a cup of coffee I set out at six o'clock to call on Timofey Semyonych, calculating that at this hour all family men with secure positions would be sitting or lying down at home.

Having written this first chapter in a manner fitting the occurrence it relates, I intend from now on to use a style perhaps not so elevated but in return more natural, of which I give the reader due warning.

II.

The worthy Timofey Semyonych greeted me rather hurriedly and apparently in some embarrassment. He conducted me into his narrow study and shut the door tight: "So as not to be bothered by the children," he explained, clearly feeling uneasy. Then he seated me in a chair, sat down himself in an armchair, drew the skirts of his old padded dressing-gown over his knees and assumed, just in case, a sort of official, even almost severe expression, though he was neither my superior nor Ivan Matveyich's, and hitherto had been reckoned an ordinary colleague and more or less an acquaintance.

"First of all," he began, "please remember that I am not a person in authority, but just the same sort of subordinate as you or Ivan Matveyich. . . In other words I am an outsider, and I don't intend to become involved."

I was surprised to see that he already seemed to know about things. Nevertheless I repeated the whole story to him in all its details. I even spoke in some agitation, for at this moment I was fulfilling the duty of a true friend. He listened to me without evincing any particular surprise, but with every sign of suspicion.

"Well, well!" he said, when he had heard me to the end. "I always expected he would end up like that."

"But why, Timofey Semyonych? It's hardly a thing one could have expected!"

"I quite agree. But ever since Ivan Timofeyich entered Government service he has been tending towards such an end. Much too smart; impudent even. Nothing but 'progress' and all sorts of wild ideas; and look where his 'progress' has landed him!"

"But it's a most exceptional occurrence, and you can't generalize on the strength of it with regard to all progressives. . . ."

"I'm not so sure. It all comes of too much culture,

believe me. People with too much culture are always poking their noses into things, and particularly where they're not wanted. However, no doubt you know better," he added, apparently rather nettled. "I can't boast of so much culture, and I'm getting on in years; I come of a military family, and I celebrated my jubilee this year."

"Don't say such things, Timofey Semyonych. On the contrary, Ivan Matveyich thirsts for your advice, your guidance. Even, as it were, with tears in his eyes."

"'As it were, with tears in his eyes.' Hm. Well, they are crocodile's tears, and not quite to be trusted. Now tell me, what on earth did he want to go abroad for? And who was going to pay for his trip? You know he hasn't a penny to his name."

"He's been saving up for a long time, Timofey Semyonych," I answered plaintively. "He only wanted to be away for three months. To see Switzerland—the birthplace of William Tell."

"William Tell? Hm."

"And he wanted to meet the spring in Naples. To view museums, and customs, and animals. . . ."

"Hm! Animals! In my opinion it was just vanity. What animals? Animals? Haven't we plenty here at home? There are zoos, and museums, and camels. There are bears just outside Petersburg. And after all, hasn't he settled down in a crocodile?"

"Timofey Semyonych, have a heart! A man's in distress, he has recourse to you as a friend, as his eldest relative, and you . . . reproach him. . . . At any rate show some sympathy for the unhappy Elena Ivanovna!"

"His wife, you mean? A charming little lady," said Timofey Semyonych, visibly affected, and taking a pinch of snuff with relish. "More in her than meets the eye, though. And so deliciously plump, and the way she keeps putting her little head on one side. . . . Charming! Andrey Osipych was talking of her only the day

F

before yesterday."

"Was he, indeed?"

"He was, and in the most flattering of terms. A marvellous figure, he said, and those eyes, and the way she does her hair. . . . Like something out of a box of chocolates, he said, and laughed. He's still quite young you know." Timofey Semyonych blew his nose sonorously. "But as for her husband, who's also quite young, a fine career he's making for himself!"

"It's anything but a question of making a career, Timofey Semyonych!"

"How true!"

"Well, what about it, then?"

"What can I do?"

"At least advise him, guide him, as a man of experience, as a relative. What is to be done? Should his superiors be approached?"

"His superiors? Don't dream of doing that," said Timofey Semyonych hastily. "If you want my advice, it's that you should try and hush the affair up, and act in a purely private capacity. The whole business is very suspicious, and highly unusual too. That's the trouble; it's so unusual, there's no precedent we can act on. . . . So one must be very careful. Let him lie there for a while. And as for us, we must wait and see."

"Wait and see, Timofey Semyonych? But supposing he goes and dies on us?"

"Why should he? Didn't you yourself say that he had settled down quite comfortably?"

I told him the whole story all over again. Timofey Semyonych pondered.

"Hm," he said at length, twiddling his snuff-box. "As I see it, it's all to the good that he should lie there for a while, instead of going abroad. It'll give him leisure to think things over. Of course, we mustn't let him suffocate; steps must be taken to ensure that his health doesn't suffer, that he doesn't catch cold or anything like that. . . . As for the German, my personal opinion is that he is entirely in the right, and even more so than the other party, for it was *his* crocodile that was entered without permission; *he* didn't enter Ivan Matveyich's crocodile without so much as by your leave. In any case, as far as I remember, Ivan Matveyich didn't own a crocodile. Well, a crocodile constitutes property, and so can't be chopped about and nothing in return."

" To save a human life, Timofey Semyonych. . . ."

" That's a matter for the police. The police should be called in."

" But think, Ivan Matveyich might be needed. They might want him in the office."

" Need Ivan Matveyich? How funny! In any case, he's supposed to be on leave, so we can ignore what has happened and behave as though he were travelling in Europe. Of course, it will be a different matter if he doesn't put in an appearance when his leave is up; then will be the time to start asking questions and initiating investigations. . . ."

" Three months! Timofey Semyonych, have a heart!"

" Well, it's his own fault. Who asked him to go rushing in there? It looks as though he'll need someone to look after him, and that's not provided for in the budget. But the chief thing is that the crocodile constitutes property, and consequently the so-called laws of economics come into play. And there's nothing more important. The other evening Ignaty Prokofyich was talking on the subject at Luke Andreyich's place. You know Ignaty Prokofyich? Quite a capitalist, in a big way of business, and knows how to put things very clearly. What we need, he said, is industry; as it is, we haven't nearly enough. It must be brought into being. Capital must be brought into being; in other words a middle class, a bourgeoisie as they call it. And as we have no capitalists they must be attracted from abroad. First of all we must encourage foreign companies to

buy up our lands in lots, as is being done everywhere
abroad. Communal property, says he, is poison, ruina-
tion! And he talks so heatedly, you know; well, it's
quite fitting, with all that wealth behind him. Not as
though he were in a Government office. . . . . While
things are run communally, he says, there's no hope for
either industry or agriculture. Foreign companies should
buy up as much of our land as they can, and then break
it up into smaller and smaller lots. And he says it so
vigorously, you know: b-r-r-reak it up, he says, and sell
the lots as private property. Or rather not sell them,
but lease them. When all the land is in the hands of
foreign companies, he says, it can be leased at any price
you like to name. In consequence the peasant will have
to work three times as hard as before, merely to earn his
daily bread; and what is more he can be driven from the
soil whenever it suits you. And he won't forget that,
and he'll be humble, and industrious, and work three
times as hard as before. Whereas under the communal
system he knows that he'll never die of hunger, and so
he just slacks and boozes. Now under the other system
capital would flow in, and a middle class would spring
up. The English political and literary paper *The Times,*
discussing our finances the other day, said that they
were in such a bad way because we had no middle
class, no big fortunes, no subservient proletariat. . . .
Ignaty Prokofyich explains everything marvellously. A
regular orator. He intends to send a paper to the
authorities, and have it published in the press. That's
the sort of thing to write, and not the silly verses Ivan
Matveyich produces. . . ."

"But what about Ivan Matveyich?" I managed to put
in, thinking the old man had chattered long enough.
Now and then Timofey liked to chatter a bit and so show
that he was in touch with affairs.

"What about Ivan Matveyich? That's just what I'm
coming to. What we're doing is trying to attract foreign

capital; and just think, no sooner is the capital of the attracted crocodile-proprietor doubled by Ivan Matveyich than we, instead of trying to encourage the foreign owner, start fussing about with designs on his capital's belly. Is that sense? In my opinion Ivan Matveyich, as a true son of the fatherland, ought to be very glad and proud at having doubled the value of a foreign crocodile, and perhaps even trebled it. That's what you must do if you hope to attract capital. If one man makes a success of it, before long another will be coming along with a crocodile, and a third will bring two or three more with him, and capital will accumulate around them. And there's your bourgeoisie. That's what must be encouraged."

"But think, Timofey Semyonych!" I cried. "You are demanding an almost supernatural degree of self-sacrifice from poor Ivan Matveyich."

"I'm not demanding anything, and I must beg you—as I have already begged you—to bear in mind that I am not a person in authority, and therefore have no right to demand anything of anybody. I am merely speaking as a patriotic Russian. And after all, who asked him to go plunging into crocodiles? A respectable fellow, endowed with a certain rank, with a charming wife, and all of a sudden . . . such a step! Is it sense?"

"But it happened quite by accident!"

"I'm not so sure. And tell me, what funds are to be drawn on to compensate the proprietor of the crocodile?"

"Ivan Matveyich's salary, perhaps."

"Would that suffice?"

"No, Timofey Semyonych," I replied sorrowfully. "The crocodile-owner was at first afraid that his crocodile would burst; but when he saw that there was nothing to fear he started putting on side, and realized to his joy that he could easily ask twice as much."

"Three times as much, four times I dare say. There will be crowds of people now, and crocodile-keepers know good business when they see it. Moreover it's carnival-time, there's a general tendency to jollification; and so, I repeat, it's necessary above all that Ivan Matveyich should remain incognito and let things take their course. Let everybody know, if you like, that he is inside the crocodile; but let them have no official cognizance of the fact. In this respect Ivan Matveyich is in an exceptionally fortunate position, since he is officially on foreign leave. Let people say he's in the crocodile; we shall know better. That's the way to arrange things. The main thing is that he should bide his time; in any case, where's the hurry?"

" But supposing . . ."

" Don't worry; he has a stout constitution . . ."

"And when he has bided his time?"

"Well, I won't conceal from you that it's an extremely ticklish case. So hard to come to a conclusion; such a nuisance that there's no sort of precedent. If there were only a precedent, we should have some idea of how to proceed. But as it is, what are we to do? And the longer we think about it the longer a decision is delayed."

A happy thought struck me.

" Couldn't we fix it this way?" I said. "If he's condemned to remain in the beast's interior and a beneficent Providence preserves his life, mightn't he perhaps put in a request to be considered on duty?"

" Hm. Possibly as on leave without pay."

" Couldn't he continue to draw his pay?"

" On what grounds?"

" As being on a special mission. . . ."

" What mission, and where to? "

" To the interior, the crocodile's interior. . . On a tour of investigation, as it were, to study the facts on the spot. Of course, it's rather novel, but it's in tune with the progressive spirit of the age, and will at the same time indicate our interest in education. . . ."

Timofey Semyonych pondered.

"To send a minor official on a special mission," he said at length, "and to study the interior of a crocodile into the bargain, is in my personal opinion the height of absurdity. Absolutely no provision for it in the budget. And in any case what could he investigate there?"

"Why, nature on the spot. Nowadays natural science is all the rage—botany and all that. . . . He'd live there for a while and communicate his observations to us. . . . Concerning the digestive system, say, or simply the creature's habits. Accumulate facts."

"I see, something of a statistical nature. Well, that's hardly in my line; I'm not a natural philosopher. You talk about accumulating facts; but as a matter of fact we're simply swamped with facts, don't know what to do with them. In any case, statistics are rather dangerous things."

"Dangerous?"

"Dangerous. Furthermore, you must agree that he will do his fact-gathering, so to speak, in a recumbent position. Now, is it possible to do Government work in a recumbent position? Another novelty, and a dangerous one at that, and absolutely lacking in precedent. Now if we could only point to one tiny little precedent, it might be possible, in my opinion, to send him on a special mission."

"For that matter live crocodiles are a novelty in this country, Timofey Semyonych."

"Hm. Quite so." He pondered again. "I don't mind admitting that your contention is justified, and might indeed furnish a basis for further action in the matter. But stop for a moment to consider what would happen, if, *pari passu* with the appearance of crocodiles, Government officials began to disappear, and further-more, in view of the warmth and softness obtaining in crocodile interiors, began to ask to be sent on special missions there, and then assumed recumbent positions. . . . Before you knew where you were everyone would be clamouring to be sent on special missions."

"Do please think of something, Timofey Semyonych! —By the way, Ivan Matveyich asked me to let you have the seven roubles he owes you from your last game of whist."

"Oh yes, that time at Nikifor Nikiforych's. I remember. To think how cheerful he was on that occasion, making us all laugh; and now. . . ."

The old man was genuinely touched.

"Please think of something!"

"I'll see what I can do. I'll have a private word with someone on the matter. In the meantime you might try to ascertain, unofficially of course, how much the proprietor would be willing to accept for his crocodile."

Timofey Semyonych was obviously growing benevolenter and benevolenter.

"I'll do so without fail," said I. "And let you know at once."

"And his poor little wife . . . all alone, I suppose? She must be missing him terribly."

"I think it would be rather nice if you could call round and see her."

"I most certainly will; I've been thinking of doing so for some time, and what better occasion could there be than this? . . . But what on earth impelled him to go and look at the crocodile? Though to tell you the truth I shouldn't mind having a look at it myself."

"Why don't you, then? You could have a word with poor Ivan Matveyich."

"I will. Of course, I don't want to rouse any false hopes by taking this step. I shall appear there in a purely private capacity.—Well, good-bye for the present. I'm going round to Nikifor Nikiforych's again. Any chance of seeing you there?"

"No. I'm going to see the captive."

"The captive, eh? The notions you have!"

I said good-bye to the old man. All sorts of thoughts

were passing through my head. It would be difficult to
find a kinder and more honest man than Timofey
Semyonych; yet as I left him I couldn't help feeling glad
that he had celebrated his jubilee, and that Timofey
Semyonyches were getting rarer and rarer. It is hardly
necessary to say that I hurried off to the Arcade to tell
poor Ivan Matveyich all that had occurred. I was also
devoured by curiosity: how was he managing in the
crocodile, how could one manage in a crocodile? At
times the whole thing seemed a monstrous dream, all
the more as it concerned a monster. . . .

III

Yet it was no dream, but genuine and indubitable
reality. Should I otherwise be narrating it? But to
resume:

It was rather late when I got to the Arcade, round
about nine o'clock, and I had to gain admission to the
crocodilery through the back entrance, for the crocodile-
keeper had closed up his establishment earlier than
usual. He was walking about at his ease in a disreput-
able old frock-coat, three times as pleased with himself
as he had been that morning. It was obvious that he felt
quite sure of his position, and that "mooch beoples
vas gumming." His Mutter came in soon after, clearly
to keep a watchful eye on me. The German kept
whispering to her. Despite the fact that the shop was
closed, he nevertheless charged me twenty-five copecks.
What repulsive pedantry!

"Each dime you vill bay; the bublic vill bay von
rouble, but I vill only charge you twenty-five gopecks,
for you are a goot vriend to your goot vriend, and I
respect vriendship."

"Is my cultured friend still alive?" I cried, approaching the crocodile and hoping that my words would
reach Ivan Matveyich from afar and flatter his vanity.

"Alive and well," he replied, as if his voice were proceeding from a great distance, or from underneath a

bed, although I was standing right next to him. " Alive and well. But of that later. How do things stand?"

Pretending not to have heard the question, I was about to inquire with eager sympathy how he was getting on inside the crocodile, what it was like being inside a crocodile, what a crocodile's inside was like, and so on. My friendship for him, nay common politeness, required that I should put these questions.

" Kindly tell me how things stand!" he cried, ordering me about as usual in his squeaky voice, which now struck me as particularly repulsive.

I recounted the whole of my conversion with Timofey Semyonych. While so doing, I endeavoured to sound rather offended.

" The old man is right," decided Ivan Matveyich, with the sharpness he always manifested when talking to me. " It's practical people I like, not sickly mumblers. I must however admit that your idea of a special commission is not totally lacking in good sense. I have much information of a scientific and moral character to communicate. But now things are taking a new and unexpected turn, and the question of salary recedes into the background. Listen attentively. Are you sitting down?"

" No, standing."

" Then kindly sit down, on the floor if need be, and attend carefully."

Angrily I took a chair and banged it down on the floor.

" Listen," he began, in a commanding tone. " There were absolutely crowds of people here to-day. Towards evening there wasn't enough room for them all, and the police had to be called in to direct the traffic. At eight o'clock, that is to say earlier than usual, the proprietor even found it necessary to shut up shop and conclude the performance, so as to be able to count the takings and make arrangements for tomorrow. Tomorrow the crowds will be bigger than ever. There's no question that all the cultured people in the capital, society ladies, foreign ambassadors, lawyers and so on, will be coming to the show. What is more, people will be coming from the countless provinces of our spacious and intriguing empire. In a word, I'm in the public eye, and occupy a pre-eminent albeit concealed position. I intend to instruct the vain masses. Taught by experience, I shall reveal myself as an example of great-hearted resignation to my lot. This will be as it were a university chair whence I shall teach mankind. The scientific information I shall be able to communicate concerning the monster I inhabit is priceless in itself. Hence, far from murmuring at what happened of late, I trust firmly in the most brilliant of careers."

"Wouldn't you find it rather boring?" I asked poisonously.

What most infuriated me was the high-and-mighty way in which he had begun to speak. Nevertheless, I felt rather taken aback. How on earth can the frivolous fellow find grounds for swanking in his pitiable condition? I whispered to myself, grinding my teeth. He should be weeping, not putting on side.

"No," he replied sharply. "For, imbued as I always have been with sublime conceptions, only now have I leisure to ponder on ameliorating the lot of all mankind. Out of a crocodile shall come light and truth. I am quite convinced that I shall discover a new theory of economic relations—a theory I shall be proud of. Hitherto I have had no time, wrapped up as I have been in my official duties and the vain pleasures of the world. I will overturn all the old ideas, and appear as a new Fourier. By the way, did you let Timofey Semyonych have his seven roubles?"

"Yes—out of my own pocket." I replied, trying to sound as though I had paid out of my own pocket.

"We'll settle up later," he said haughtily. "I'm expecting an increase in salary at any moment; for whose

salary should be increased if not mine? Think how in-
valuable I'm going to be. But to business. The wife?"

"You mean Elena Ivanovna, I suppose?"

"The wife?!" he cried—even screeched.

There was no help for it. Humbly, but nevertheless
grinding my teeth, I told him how I had left Elena
Ivanovna. But he didn't even let me finish.

"I have special plans for her," he said impatiently.
"If I am to be famous *here,* I want her to be famous
there. Scientists, philosophers, foreign geologists, states-
men, after conversing with me in the morning will visit
her salon in the evening. Beginning with next week she
must hold salons every evening. My increase in salary
will cover arrangements for the receptions, particularly as
the expenses will be limited to tea and hired lackeys.
Both here and there people will talk of me. I have long
been anxious to have people talk of me, but could never
achieve this aim, hampered by my low rank and lack
of significance. Now all this has been achieved through
a mere swallow by a crocodile. My every word will be
listened to, my every pronouncement thought about,
handed on, published. And I'll have plenty to say, never
fear! At last they will realize what qualities they
permitted to disappear into the interior of a crocodile.
'This man might have conducted foreign affairs, or ruled
a kingdom,' some will say. 'And this man didn't conduct foreign affairs or rule a kingdom,' others will say.
Now in what way am I inferior to a Garnier-Pagèsky, or
whatever his name is? And the wife must form a pen-
dant to me. Mine the mind, hers the beauty and charm.
'She is beautiful, and so she is his wife,' some will say.
'She is beautiful *because* she is his wife,' others will say.
In any case let Elena Ivanovna buy an encyclopaedia tomorrow, so as to be able to discuss everything. But above
all let her read the *Petersburg News,* checking every day
with *The Hair.* I am assuming that the proprietor of my
crocodile will sometimes consent to convey me, together

with my reptilian host, to my wife's brilliant salon. I shall
lie there in the crocodile-box, sprinkling impromptu witti-
cisms prepared that morning. To the statesman I will
communicate my projects; to the poet I will discourse in
rhyme; to the ladies I will be amusing and morally
charming—since presenting no sort of danger for their
husbands. For the rest I shall serve as an example of
submission to fate and the will of Providence. I will
make my wife a shining light in literary circles; I'll bring
her out and explain her to the public; as my wife, she
must be dignified and distinguished, and if they are right
to call Andrey Alexandrovich our Russian Alfred de
Musset, they will be even more justified in calling her
the Russian Eugénie Tour."

I must confess that though this was the sort of nonsense that Ivan Matveyich was in the habit of talking, it
occurred to me that he was delirious. It was the Ivan
Matveyich of every day, but as though looked at through
a glass magnifying twenty times.

"My friend," I said, "do you expect to attain a great
age? And generally speaking, is your health all right?
How's your sleeping, your breathing? I am your friend,
and this is, you must agree, a most unusual occurrence;
and consequently my curiosity is only natural."

"It's sheer curiosity nevertheless," he replied ponder-
ously. "But it shall be satisfied. You want to know
how I have settled down in the interior of the crocodile?
In the first place, to my great surprise, the crocodile
proved to be quite hollow. Its inside consists so to speak
of elastic material, rather like those articles on sale in
Gorokhovaya Street, in Morskaya Street and, if I am
not mistaken, on the Voznesensky Prospekt. Otherwise,
how would there be room for me?"

"Is it possible?" I cried in natural surprise. "Can
the crocodile be completely hollow?"

"It can and is," Ivan Matveyich confirmed, sternly and
emphatically. "And in all probability it is so con-

structed in accordance with the laws of Nature. The crocodile merely possesses a pair of jaws equipped with sharp teeth, and in addition a tail of considerable length —and that, in effect, is all. In the middle, between these two extremities, there is an empty expanse surrounded by something in the nature of rubber, something which in all probability is in fact really rubber."

"And what about its ribs, and its stomach, and its intestines, and its liver, and its heart?"

"It has nothing of the sort—absolutely nothing; and in all probability never had. Any assertions to the contrary are merely the vain fancies of frivolous travellers. Just as you inflate an air-cushion, so I am at the present moment inflating the crocodile. It is incredibly dilatable. Even you, as a friend of the family, would have room to lie down at my side, if you had the magnanimity to come in; and still there would be room to spare. I am even thinking, if things come to the point, of inviting Elena Ivanovna to join me. In any case, a similar inward hollowness is perfectly in agreement with the teachings of science. For supposing you were assigned the task of constructing a crocodile, the first question that would naturally arise would be: What is the function of the crocodile? And the answer is clear: To swallow people. How may the crocodile be best contrived to perform the function of swallowing people? The answer is still clearer: By making it hollow inside. Physics long ago discovered that Nature abhors a vacuum. Accordingly, the interior of a crocodile must constitute a vacuum, so that, being abhorred, it may be filled up with anything that comes to hand—or rather jaw. There you have the sole sensible reason why crocodiles are so prone to swallow us. The human arrangement is, of course, somewhat different; the emptier, for instance, a human head is, the less it feels any compulsion to fill itself; but this is the sole exception to the general rule. All this is now as clear as day; all this I have achieved thanks to my intel-

ligence and experience, being as it were in the bosom of
Nature, in Nature's retort, listening to the beating of
Nature's pulse. The very etymology of the word supports
me, for the name crocodile means voracity. Crocodile,
Crocodillo, is clearly an Italian word, contemporary no
doubt with the ancient Pharaohs of Egypt, and indubit-
ably deriving from the French root *croquer,* meaning
to eat up, feed on and generally employ for alimentary
purposes.   On all this I intend to lecture at my first
gathering in Elena Ivanovna's salon, when they have
conveyed me there in the box."

"My friend, don't you think you ought to take a laxa-
tive?" I could not prevent myself from crying. He's
in a fever, I repeated to myself in horror.

"What nonsense!" he replied scornfully. "And in
any case what could be more inconvenient in view of my
present position? Though I more or less knew that you
would bring up the subject of laxatives."

"But, my dear friend, how . . . how are you taking
your nourishment? Have you dined to-day?"

"No, but I feel quite comfortable inside, and in all
probability shall never take nourishment again. That
too is quite understandable. Filling as I do the whole
interior of the crocodile, I maintain it in a condition of
permanent satiety. It won't need to be fed for years.
On the other hand, sated with me, it will naturally
communicate to me the vital juices from its body ; it's
rather like the way in which certain refined coquettes
cover themselves up at night with raw cutlets and then,
after their morning bath, appear fresh, resilient, succulent and engaging. In this way, feeding the crocodile
on myself, I in turn receive my nourishment from it; in
a word, we feed one another reciprocally. But as it is
difficult, even for a crocodile, to digest a man such as
I, it must of course feel a certain uneasiness in the
stomach—which, for that matter, it doesn't possess—and
that is the reason why, in order not to cause the monster

unnecessary suffering, I rarely turn from side to side; I
could easily do so, but my humanity bids me refrain.
That is the sole drawback to my present position, and
in the allegorical sense Timofey is right to refer to my
recumbent position. But I will prove that even in that
position—nay, only in that position is it possible to transform the fate of mankind. All the great ideas and trends
of our newspapers and journals have been produced by
people in, so to speak, a recumbent position; that is
precisely the reason why such ideas and trends are called
star-gazing; but who cares what they are called? I shall
invent a whole new system of philosophy, and you'll
never believe how easily. All you need to do is to with-
draw into some remote corner, say into the interior of a
crocodile, close your eyes, and in a trice you've devised
a whole paradise for the human race. When you left
me the other day I set about inventing systems, and I
have already invented three and am engaged on a fourth.
It's true that first of all you have to refute all the other
systems; but it's so easy to refute when you're inside a
crocodile; in fact, from here everything seems to become
clearer. . . . However, there are in fact certain other
drawbacks attached to my position, though only minor
ones: the inside of a crocodile is dampish and apparently
covered with some sort of slime, and moreover it smells
rather of India-rubber, just like my last year's goloshes.
But that's all; there are no other drawbacks."

"Ivan Matveyich," I interrupted, "all these are marvels
which I find it hard to believe. And can it be true that
you intend never again to dine."

"What nonsensical trifles you bother about, you
frivolous and empty-headed fellow! I am expounding
my sublime ideas, and you. . . . Know then that I am
sufficienty nourished by the great ideas shining through
the night in which I am enveloped. However, the good-
natured proprietor of the monster, by arrangement with
his venerable Mutter, has agreed that every morning a

metal tube shall be inserted in the crocodile's mouth, and through it I shall be able to take in coffee, or broth with white bread crumbled in it. The metal tube has already been ordered from a neighbouring establishment, but for my part I consider it a superfluous luxury. As for the length of my life, I hope to exist for at least a thousand years, if it be true that crocodiles live that long; I should be obliged if you would check the point tomorrow in some work of natural history and let me know if I am right, for I may have confused the crocodile with some other fossil. There is only one consideration that somewhat perturbs me. Being dressed as I am in cloth garments and having boots on my feet, the crocodile will not be able to digest me. In addition, I am alive, and hence in a position to resist digestion with the whole of my will-power; and you can easily understand that I do not wish to be converted into what all food is converted into—that would really be too humiliating. But I am afraid of one thing: in the course of a thousand years the fabric of my clothes, unfortunately of Russian manufacture, may disintegrate, and then, being unclothed, despite all my natural indignation I may find myself being digested; and though in the daytime I should never think of permitting it, at night, when I am asleep, when my will lies dormant, I may suffer the undignified fate of a potato, a pancake or a piece of veal. The very idea revolts me. For this reason alone we ought to alter our tariff laws and encourage the import of English materials, which are stouter, and therefore more capable of resisting the forces of Nature if their wearer happens to find himself inside a crocodile. I shall begin by communicating my idea to someone in authority, and at the same time to the political correspondents of our Petersburg dailies. Let them voice it. I trust that it will not be the only idea they will borrow from me. I can foresee that every morning crowds of them, armed with quarter-roubles from the petty cash, will surge around me, anxious to hear my reactions to yesterday's cables. To put it briefly, the future appears to me in the rosiest of lights."

"He's raving," I whispered to myself.

"And what about freedom, my friend?" I asked, wishing to learn his views on all subjects. "You are, so to speak, in a dungeon, whereas a human ought to enjoy freedom."

"Don't be stupid! Savages love independence, wise folk love order. And order doesn't exist. . . ."

"For goodness' sake, Ivan Matveyich. . . ."

"Be silent and attend!" he squeaked, vexed by my interruption. "Never before have I soared so through the realms of the spirit. In my narrow retreat there is only one thing I fear: the literary criticism of the fat periodicals and the jeering whistle of our satirical journals. I fear lest frivolous visitors, the foolish and the jealous, the nihilists generally, may make a laughing-stock of me. But I will take steps. I am impatient to hear the reactions of the crowd tomorrow, and above all the views of the papers. You must tell me what the papers say tomorrow."

"Very well; I'll bring a whole pile of them."

"Perhaps tomorow would be rather early, for reports are always printed four days late. But from now on you must come every evening, through the back door. I intend to employ you as my secretary. You will read the papers and journals to me, and I will dictate my thoughts and issue my instructions. And above all don't forget the foreign cables. Every day they must all reach me. But enough for now; I expect you want to go to bed. Run along home, and forget what I said just now about criticism; I am not afraid of it, for criticism itself is in a highly critical position. All you need to be is wise and virtuous, and people cannot but put you on a pedestal. If not a Socrates, then at least a Diogenes, or both to-gether; such shall be my rôle in the history of mankind."

With such frivolous importunity (it is true he was in

a fever) did Ivan Matveyich hasten to pour out his heart to me, just like those weak-willed women who, as the saying goes, can't keep a thing to themselves. And everything that he had told me about the crocodile struck me as being highly suspicious. How was it possible that the crocodile should be quite hollow inside? I was ready to bet that he'd said so simply out of vanity, and to some extent in order to humiliate me. He was ill, of course; and one must make allowances for the sick; but I will confess that I had never been able to bear Ivan Matveyich. All my life, from my earliest years, I had wished, and been unable, to escape from his tutelage. A thousand times I had wished to give him a piece of my mind and leave him for ever, and every time something seemed to draw me back to him, as though there were something I still hoped to be able to prove to him, some sort of vengeance I could wreak on him. A strange thing was our friendship! I can honestly say that nine-tenths of my friendship for him was due to irritation. This time, however, we parted on fairly good terms.

"Your vriend is a very glever man," said the German to me in a low voice, as he was seeing me off the premises; all the time he had been earnestly following our conversation.

"By the way," I said, "before I forget: How much would you accept for your crocodile, supposing someone wished to purchase it?"

Ivan Matveyich, who had overheard the question, waited curiously for the answer. It was clear that he did not want the German to accept too little; at any rate, he gave a significant grunt when he heard my question.

At first the German refused to consider the proposal; he even grew angry.

"No one shall buy mine own grogodile!" he cried furiously, turning as red as a lobster. "I do not vish to sell mine grogodile. Today I gollect von hundred thirty talers from the bublic, tomorrow I gollect ten thousand talers, the next day von hundred thousand talers, and then every day von hundred thousand talers I gollect. I vill not sell."

Ivan Matveyich even gave a giggle of pleasure.

Forcing myself to be cool and reasonable—for I was performing the duty of a true friend—I hinted to the crazy Teuton that he was somewhat out in his reckoning; that if every day he collected ten thousand, in four days the whole of Petersburg would have passed through his establishment, and then there would be no one to collect from any more; that life and death lay in the hands of God, and that his crocodile might suddenly burst, or Ivan Matveyich fall ill and die, and so on and so forth.

The German thought for a while.

"I vill give him drops from the ghemist's," he said, when he had finished thinking. "Then your vriend vill not die."

"Drops are all very well as far as they go," said I; "but supposing there's a lawsuit? Ivan Matveyich's wife may demand her legal husband. You are planning to get rich, but are you planning to pay Elena Ivanovna a pension for life?"

"I am not blanning!" said the German firmly and sternly.

"He is not blanning!" repeated his Mutter, quite viciously.

"Well then, wouldn't it be better for you to accept a lump sum, if only a modest sum, but concrete and reliable, rather than put your trust in an uncertain future? I feel it my duty to add that I am asking purely out of curiosity."

The German took his Mutter aside and conferred with her in the corner where stood the cupboard with the largest and most hideous of all the monkeys.

"You just wait and see!" said Ivan Matveyich.

As for me, I was at this moment burning with the desire first of all to give the German a sound thrashing, secondly to give his Mutter an even sounder one, and thirdly to give Ivan Matveyich the soundest thrashing of all for his boundless vanity. But all this faded into insignificance before the demand of the avid German.

Having conferred with his Mutter, he demanded for his crocodile fifty thousand roubles in tickets of the last internal loan, with lottery, a stone-built house on Gorokhovaya Street, to include his own private chemist's shop, and in addition the rank of colonel in the Russian army.

"You see?" cried Ivan Matveyich in triumph. "What did I tell you? Save for his last senseless desire to be promoted colonel, he is absolutely right; for he fully understands the present worth of the crocodile he is exhibiting. The laws of economic *über alles!*"

"Good heavens!" I cried to the German. "What do you want to be a colonel for? What feat of arms have you performed, what military glory have you achieved? You must be crazy to suggest such a thing!"

"Grazy?" cried the German, offended. "'I am not grazy; I am a very glever man, and you are very stupid. I deserve to be a golonel because I have exhibit von grogodile, and in that grogodile inside is a live *Hofrat!* I am a very glever man, and very mooch do I vish to be a golonel."

"Good-bye then, Ivan Matveyich!" I cried, trembling with fury, and almost at a run I ran out of the crocodilery. I felt that in another minute I shouldn't be able to answer for myself. The unnatural hopes of the two blockheads were simply unbearable. The fresh air cooled my heated brow and somewhat quelled my indignation. At length, having spat vigorously some fifteen times on either side, I took a cab, drove home, undressed, and threw myself on my bed. The most vexing thing of all was that I had found myself engaged as his secretary. Now I should have to go there and die of boredom every evening, performing the duties of a true friend. I felt like kicking myself for having permitted it, and in fact,

having put out the candle and drawn the sheet over me,
I struck myself several times with my fist on the head
and other parts of the body. This somewhat relieved
me, and at last I fell asleep, fairly soundly even, for I
was extremely tired. All night I dreamt of nothing but
monkeys, but towards morning I also dreamt of Elena
Ivanovna. . . .

IV

I presume that I dreamt about monkeys because of
those I had seen at the crocodilery; but Elena Ivanovna
was another kettle of fish.

I will say at once that I loved the lady; but I hasten
at full speed to add that I loved her as a father, neither
more nor less. I conclude that this was the nature of
my affection because I had frequently been filled with
an irresistible desire to kiss her on her brow or her little
pink cheek. And though I had never achieved this
desire, I must confess that I should not have refused to
kiss her on her lips. Nay, not merely on her lips, but
on her little teeth, which so charmingly came into view,
just like a row of pretty little pearls, every time she
laughed. And she laughed with amazing frequency.
When he was feeling affectionate, Ivan Matveyich used to
call her his " dear absurdity," and this was an appella-
tion in the highest degree fitting and significant. She
was a little bonbon of a lady, and nothing more. This
is why I completely fail to understand how the same Ivan
Matveyich should suddenly have thought of picturing his
wife as a Russian Eugénie Tour. Be that as it may, my
dreams, apart from the monkeys, made the pleasantest
of impressions on me, and going over in my head, as I
was taking a morning cup of tea, the events of the preceding day, I resolved to call on her on my way to the
office, which in any case I ought to do in my capacity
of friend of the family.

In the tiny room next to the bedroom, in what they
called their small drawing-room, though their large

drawing-room was equally exiguous, on a little divan, at a little tea-table, in some sort of ethereal négligé, sat Elena Ivanovna, taking coffee from a tiny cup in which she was dipping a minute cracknel. She was entrancingly pretty, but also struck me as being rather pensive.

" Ah, it's you, you naughty man," she greeted me, with an absent-minded smile. " Sit down, you giddy thing, and have some coffee. Well, what did you do yesterday? Were you at the masked ball?"

" D'you mean you were?! I'm not going to such things these days . . . and in any case I was visiting our poor captive. . . ."

I sighed, and assumed a regretful expression as I sipped my coffee.

" Who? What captive? Oh yes! The poor boy! Well, how's he getting on? Feeling terribly bored? By the way, I wanted to ask you. . . . I could get a divorce now, couldn't I?"

" A divorce?" I cried indignantly, almost spilling my coffee. It's that dark-complexioned fellow, I said to myself furiously.

There was a certain dark-complexioned individual with a little moustache serving in the building department, who kept visiting them really too often and was terribly good at making Elena Ivanovna laugh. I must confess that I absolutely loathed him, and I didn't doubt for a moment that he had managed to see Elena Ivanovna at the masked ball, or perhaps even here, and filled her head with all sorts of nonsense.

" After all," Elena Ivanovna went on quickly, obviously repeating a lesson, " if he's going to be stuck there in the cwocodile and perhaps never come home again, am I supposed to sit here and wait? A husband should live at home and not in a cwocodile. . . ."

" But it was such an unforeseen occurrence . . . ." I began, in natural agitation.

" Don't say such things; I won't listen!" she cried,

quite angry now. "You always take sides against me, you cwuel thing! Never help me in the least. Even outsiders are telling me that I have gwounds for a divorce, since Ivan Matveyich won't weceive his salawy any more."

"Elena Ivanovna? Can you really be saying such things?" I cried pathetically. "What scoundrel can have been putting these ideas in your head? A divorce on such flimsy grounds as cessation of salary is absolutely unthinkable. And poor Ivan Matveyich is, so to speak, fainting for love of you, even there in the monster's interior. Melting away with love, like a lump of sugar. Only last evening, while you no doubt were enjoying yourself at the masked ball, he was telling me that if things came to the point he intended to summon you, as his legal wife, to join him in the interior, particularly as the crocodile has proved to be extremely capacious, and would provide room not merely for two but even for three. . . ."

And I related to her the whole of this interesting part of my conversation with Ivan Matveyich the evening before.

"What!" she cried, absolutely flabbergasted. "You want me to cwawl in there to join Ivan Matveyich? The idea! As though I could, in my bonnet and cwinoline! What fantastic nonsense! And what sort of spectacle should I pwesent while cwawling in, supposing someone were watching . . . ? It's simply widiculous! And what should I have to eat there? And how should I manage if. . . . Goodness gwacious, what an idea! And what sort of amusements could I hope for? You say the whole place smells of India-wubber? And supposing we were to quawwel, should I have to stay there at his side? How beastly!"

"I agree, I absolutely agree with all you say, dear Elena Ivanovna," I hastened to interrupt, filled with the natural urge to express oneself that always overcomes one

when one thinks that one has right on one's side. " But
you forget one thing. You forget that he cannot live
without you, that he is calling to you, his heart filled
with love, passionate love, overwhelming love. . . .
You have forgotten about love, dear Elena Ivanovna."

" I wefuse to listen to another word," she cried, waving her pretty little hand, on which the freshly polished
nails gleamed pinkly. " You're simply unbeawable.
You'll make me cwy in a minute. Cwawl in there yourself if you want to. You're his fwiend, so go and lie
down with him, and you can spend all the west of your
lives arguing about some dull scientific point. . . ."

" You are wrong to ridicule the suggestion," I soberly
checked the impulsive woman. " As a matter of fact,
Ivan Matveyich invited me too. Of course, it is your
wifely duty that beckons you there, whereas I should
merely be following the promptings of my heart; but
when he was telling me about the dilatability of the
crocodile Ivan Matveyich hinted quite plainly that there
would be room not merely for the two of you but for me
as well, in my capacity of friend of the family; room for
all three of us, and that if I cared . . . "

" What, the thwee of us?" cried Elena Ivanovna, looking at me in amazement. " So the thwee of us would
lie there together? Ha-ha-ha! How stupid the pair of
you are! Ha-ha-ha! I'd spend all my time pinching you,
you naughty man, ha-ha-ha-ha-ha!"

And leaning back on the divan she laughed till the tears
came into her eyes. Everything about her, tears and
laughter, was so entrancing that I couldn't resist, and bent
over to kiss her hand. She offered no resistance, though
she tweaked me slightly by the ears to show that we were
friends again.

We grew quite hilarious, and I told her all about Ivan
Matveyich's plans. She found the idea of evening receptions and the holding of a salon highly attractive.

" But I shall need ever so many new fwocks," she remarked, "and so Ivan Matveyich must send his salawy along as soon as possible . . . But as for . . . as for his being bwought along in the cwocodile-box," she added thoughtfully, "I'm not at all sure. . . . No, it would be too too widiculous! I don't want my husband to be bwought along in a box. I should feel so embawwassed before all the visitors. . . No, I won't have it!"

"By the way, did Timofey Semyonych call on you yesterday evening?"

"He did; he came to cheer me up, and just think, we spent the whole time playing double-dummy whist. He paid his losses in sweets, and if I lost he kissed my hand. Such a naughty man, and just think, he nearly came to the masked ball with me!"

"Quite carried away, I see!" I observed. "And who wouldn't be—by you, you delightful creature?"

"There you go with your absurd compliments! Come here, I'll pinch you good-bye. I'm terribly good at pinching. There, how did you like that? By the way, you say Ivan Matveyich talked about me a lot yesterday?"

"Well, perhaps not a lot. . . . I must confess that he seemed more interested in the fate of mankind, and is planning . . ."

"Let him plan! Don't say anything more about it; I'm sure it's shockingly dull. But I must call wound and see him. I'll go tomowwow; can't go today—I have a slight headache, and there will be so many people. . . . They'll say: That's his wife. Most embawwassing! By-bye then! This evening you'll be there, eh?"

"I shall. He asked me to take the papers along."

"Well, that's fine. Pop along and wead them to him. And don't come back here afterwards. I'm not feeling well, and I may perhaps call on some people. By-bye, you naughty boy!"

That dark-complexioned fellow is coming this evening, I thought to myself.

At the office, needless to say, I gave no sign of the

anxieties and cares that were devouring me. But I soon noticed that some of our more progressive papers were passing that morning from hand to hand with more than usual speed, and being studied by my colleagues with exceptionally serious expressions. The first that came my way was *The Leaflet,* a little paper lacking in any special trend, just vaguely humanitarian, for which reason my colleagues tended to despise it, though they read it often enough. Not without pleasure I read in it the following:

" Yesterday in our capital of wide expanses and magnificent architecture extraordinary rumours were rife. A certain N., a well-known upper-class gourmet, no doubt having wearied of the cuisine at Borel's and the ———— Club, was said to have gone into the Arcade, proceeded to the spot where an enormous crocodile that had just been brought from foreign parts was on show, and demanded that it should be dished up as his dinner. Having struck a bargain with the beast's owner, he there and then commenced to devour it while it was still alive, cutting off succulent morsels with his penknife and hurriedly swallowing them. Bit by bit the whole of the crocodile vanished into the connoisseur's capacious inside; and when he had finished he even expressed a desire to follow it up with the ichneumon that shared the crocodile's box, no doubt assuming that ichneumon-steak would be equally appetizing. We are far from objecting to this addition to our menu; we have long felt, as our readers will remember, that it would soon appear on our tables, particularly as it has long been a favourite of foreign gourmets. English lords and travellers organize regular crocodile-hunts in Egypt and prepare choice cuts from the monster with mustard, onions and potatoes. The French, arriving in Egypt with de Lesseps, found that they preferred the beast's paws, which they boil on hot ashes, so doing in fact to spite the English, who make fun of them. No doubt we shall find merits in both ways of preparing the meat. And for our part we are pleased at this new branch

of industry, which has hitherto been lacking in our powerful and many-sided fatherland. Before a year has elapsed
from the disappearance of this first crocodile into the
interior of the Petersburg gourmet, we have no doubt that
the creature will be rife in Russia. And why should they
not become acclimatized to our country? If the waters
of the Neva are too cold for these interesting visitors,
there are after all pools in the capital, and rivers and lakes
outside it. Why not breed them there? Providing our
connoisseurs with an agreeable and wholesome dish, they
might at the same time serve to amuse the ladies boating
on the ponds and to instruct the children in natural history. From crocodile-leather trunks, cigarette-cases and
wallets might be contrived, and no doubt more than one
bundle of a thousand roubles, in the greasy notes that our
merchants appear to fancy, would be snugly tucked away
in crocodile-skin. We intend to revert to this interesting
subject."

Though I had rather expected something of the sort,
nevertheless the precipitancy of the announcement took
me somewhat aback. Wishing to share my impressions,
I turned to Prokhor Savvich, who was sitting opposite me;
I realized that he was looking at me and that he held
The Hair in his hand, as though wishing to effect an exchange. Silently he took from me *The Leaflet,* and as
he handed me *The Hair* he scored with his finger-nail an
article to which he presumably wished to draw my attention. This Prokhor Savvich was the queerest of individuals: a taciturn old bachelor, he entered into no
relations with us, spoke to hardly anyone in the office,
always had his own opinion on every topic, but couldn't
bear to pass it on to anyone else. He lived a solitary existence. Hardly any of us had ever been to his place.

This is what I read in *The Hair* :

" As is well known, we are progressive and humanitarian, and anxious to emulate Europe in these respects.
But despite all our strivings and the efforts of our daily

press, we are far from having succeeded, as witness the
revolting occurrence of which the Arcade was yesterday
the scene, an occurrence which, our readers will recall,
we had foreshadowed more than once. A foreigner comes
to our capital, bringing with him a crocodile, which he
begins to exhibit to the public in the Arcade. We hasten
to welcome this new branch of industry, which our powerful and many-sided fatherland has hitherto lacked.
Suddenly, at half past four yesterday afternoon, there
appears at the exhibition an individual of extreme obesity
and in an advanced stage of intoxication, who pays the
entrance-fee and forthwith, uttering no word as to his
design, crawls into the jaws of the crocodile, who is naturally forced to swallow him in mere self-defence, so as not
to suffocate. Having thus forced his way into the crocodile's interior the individual falls fast asleep. Neither the
cries of the crocodile's owner, nor the wails of his frightened dependents, nor the threats to call in the police, make
any impression on the intruder. All that can be heard
from the crocodile's inside are bursts of raucous laughter
and the promise to settle affairs with a whip; and the poor
mammal, forced to swallow such an enormous mass, sheds
unavailing tears. An uninvited guest is worse than a
Tartar, but despite the proverb the impudent intruder
refuses to come out. We are at a loss to explain such
barbaric actions, which bear witness to our lack of maturity
and lower us in the eyes of foreigners. Here is a fine
example of the wide Russian soul at work! One may
well ask what the uninvited visitor was after? A warm
and comfortable abode? But there are in our capital many
handsome houses providing comfortable and inexpensive
flats, with Neva water laid on, gas on the stairs, and in
many cases a uniformed janitor. Once more we must
draw our readers' attention to our barbaric treatment of
domestic animals. The visiting crocodile in question
naturally finds it difficult to digest so huge a mass, and
there it lies swollen up like a mountain, suffering agony

as it awaits its end. In Europe those who ill-treat domestic
animals have long been prosecuted by the authorities.
but despite our European lighting, our European paving,
our European house-planning, we are far from having re-
nounced our ancient traditions :

Our houses new, our prejudices old—

and for that matter our houses are not so very new, at any
rate the staircases. We have mentioned more than once
that on the Petersburg Side, in the house of the merchant
Lukyanov, the wooden back-staircase has rotted away and
collapsed in parts, and has long constituted a menace to
the soldier's wife Afimya Skapidarova in his service, who
is frequently called upon to go up or down these stairs
with water or bundles of fire-wood. At last our predic-
tions have been fulfilled. At eight-thirty p.m. yesterday,
Afimya Skapidarova fell through the stairs with a soup-
tureen in her hands, and broke her leg. We do not know
whether the merchant Lukyanov will now mend his stair-
case; Russians are good at locking the stable door when
the stallion has been purloined; however that may be,
the fact remains that his victim has been conveyed to hospital. We must similarly keep emphasizing that house-
porters on the Vyborg Side, when brushing the mud from
the wooden pavements, really must refrain from splashing
the lower garment of those passing; they should collect
the mud in neat piles, as is done in Europe. . . ."

"Whatever does this mean?" I said, looking at
Prokhor Savvich in some surprise.

"What does what mean?"

"Why, that instead of feeling sorry for Ivan Matveyich,
they feel sorry for the crocodile . . ."

"What of it? He's a mammal, isn't he? And they're
always very sorry for crocodiles in Europe. He-he!"

Saying this, queer old Prokhor Savvich plunged his
nose in his documents and uttered not another word.

I slipped *The Hair* and *The Leaflet* into my pocket, and
also collected as many other papers as I could for Ivan

Matveyich's amusement that evening. And though evening was still some way off, I slipped out of the office earlier than usual so as to get to the Arcade and watch from a distance what was going on, listen to the opinions expressed and hear the views aired. I felt that there would be an enormous crowd, and so as to be prepared I covered my face with the collar of my overcoat; for some reason I felt very reluctant to be recognized. This shows how unused we are to publicity. But I feel that I am not entitled to dilate on my own prosaic sentiments, in view of the remarkable and original nature of the occurrence I have narrated.

NIKOLAI LESKOV

THE FLEA

THE TALE OF THE LEFT-HANDED TULA SMITH WHO SQUINTED

Chapter One

WHEN the Emperor Alexander Pavlovich had concluded the Council of Vienna he took it into his Imperial head to travel through Europe and view the wonders in the various countries. He visited every one, and in each, thanks to his kindly nature, he had the most internecine conversations with all sorts and conditions of people. And in every country they had something to surprise him with, endeavouring to incline him to their side; but the whole of the time he was accompanied by the Don Cossack Platov, who viewed these efforts with a jaundiced eye and, missing his home, kept trying to lure the Emperor back. And the moment Platov noticed that the Emperor was particularly interested in some foreign gadget, the rest of his suite would be silent, but Platov would up and say: So and so, but at home we've got things as good; and in one way or other distract the Emperor's attention.

The English knew all about this, and in preparation for the Emperor's visit they had thought up all sorts of cunning devices, planning to captivate him by their foreignness and draw him away from the Russians; and on many occasions they achieved their aim, particularly at their large receptions, where Platov was unable to express himself in French with complete fluidity—not that he minded much, for he was a married man, and considered all French conversations as so much taradiddle and unworthy of the imagination. But when the English began to invite the Emperor to all sorts of arsenals, armament-works and soap-sawing factories, wishing to show their superiority over us in all respects and put on side, Platov said to himself:

" So far and no further. Hitherto I have put up with it, but this is the end. Whether I can talk French or not, I won't let my own folk down."

And hardly had he thought this than the Emperor graciously addressed him:

" So on and so forth, tomorrow we two are going to see the curio-cabinet at their armament-works. There," says he, " there are such perfections of Nature that when you've seen them you won't be able any longer to deny that the significance of us Russians is resolutely insignificant."

Platov made no reply, but just sank his gnarled nose in his shaggy felt cloak and returning to his quarters ordered his batman to fetch from his kitbag a bottle of

Caucasian vodka, swallowed a large glassful, said his
prayers at a folding prayer-stool, covered himself up in
his felt cloak and began to snore so violently that not an
Englishman in the house had a wink of sleep.

He had thought: This is a matter that must be slept
on.

Chapter Two

Next day the Emperor and Platov went to visit the
curio-cabinets. The Emperor took no other Russian with
him, for there was only room for two in the carriage that
had been provided.

They drive up to a smallish building—the entrance
unpainted, the corridors endless, all the rooms exactly
alike, and finally, in the principal hall, various enormous
bustres and in the middle, beneath a canoby, stands a
Pal o' Bill de Vere.

The Emperor looks round at Platov, to see whether he's
very surprised and what he is looking at; and Platov is
walking about, his eyes on the floor, just as though he
can't see anything, blowing rings in his whiskers.

The English at once begin to show them various
astonishments, explaining what they have contrived and
to what end, with a view to military operations: naval
stormometers, caramel-hair cloaks for the infantry, and
for the cavalry tarred mackintoshes. The Emperor is
delighted with everything he sees, everything seems splendid to him, but Platov makes it quite devious that nothing
has any interest for him.

The Emperor says:

" How is it possible for you to be so insensible? Is
there nothing here to surprise you?"

And Platov replies:

" The only thing that surprises me is that my lads from
the Don went to war without all this junk and repelled
the ten tongues and two."

The Emperor says:

" This is senseless."

H

Platov replies:

"I don't know what your Majesty considers senseless, but I dare not argue and must hold my tongue."

But the English, seeing the Emperor engaged in Russian conversation, straight away led him up to a Pal o' Bill de Vere, taking from one of its hands a Mortimer gun and from the other a pistol.

"Here," they say, "is a sample of our productivity." And they hand him the gun.

The Emperor looked calmly at the Mortimer gun, for he had some of the same sort at Tsarskoye Selo; and so they handed him the pistol, saying:

"This pistol is of synonymous and matchless handicraft; our Admiral snatched it from the belt of the bandit hetman in Candelabria."

The Emperor looked at the pistol, and couldn't stop looking.

He gave several gasps of amazement.

"Ach, ach, ach!" he gasped. "How is it conceivable . . . how is it possible that anyone should produce such delicate work?" And he turns to Platov in Russian and says: "If I had but one such craftsman in Russia I should be very very happy and proud, and without delay I'd make him a nobleman."

At these words Platov plunges his right hand into his wide trousers and brings out a screwdriver for unscrewing firearms. The English say: "It doesn't undo"; but he, paying no attention, sets about tinkering with the lock. He twisted it this way, twisted it that way—and the lock came out. Platov showed the Emperor the trigger, and on it, on the very band, was an inscription in Russian: "Ivan Moskvin in the city of Tula."

The English are amazed, and keep nudging one another:

"Cripes, there's a show-up for you!"

But the Emperor says sadly to Platov:

"Why did you confound them so? Now I feel very

sorry for them. Let us be going."

The two took their seats in the same two-seater and drove off, and that day the Emperor was at a ball, and Platov swallowed an even larger glass of vodka and slept his sound Cossack sleep.

He felt both glad that he had confounded the English and brought renown to the Tula craftsman, and also vexed: Why in such a contingency had the Emperor felt sorry for the Englishmen?

"What there was to suppress the Emperor," thought Platov, "I simply can't conceive." And thinking these thoughts he had to get out of bed twice, cross himself and drink some vodka before he was able to fall soundly asleep.

And at this time the English were also not asleep; they couldn't forget what had happened. While the Emperor was making merry at the ball, they fixed up another surprise for him that quite took the stuffing out of Platov.

Chapter Three

Next day when Platov came to say good-morning to the Emperor the latter said to him:

"Let them harness the two-seater this minute; we are going to visit some more curio-cabinets."

Platov plucked up enough courage to ask whether they hadn't perhaps already seen enough foreign products, and whether it wasn't perhaps time to think about going back home. But the Emperor says:

"No; it is my wish to view further novelties. They boast that they produce sugar of a most excellent quality."

Off they drove.

The English show the Emperor everything: what excellent articles they have; and Platov looks and looks, and suddenly says:

"And show us *molvo* sugar of your fabrication!"

But the English do not know what molvo means. They whisper to one another, wink at one another, keep repeat-

ing to one another " molvo, molvo," and can't imagine
what sort of sugar this may be; and in the end they have
to confess that they have all kinds of sugar, but not molvo.

Platov says:

" Then you have nothing to boast of. You come to our
country, and we'll give you tea to drink with genuine
molvo from the Bobrinsky factory."

But the Emperor tugged him by the sleeve and
whispered:

" I must beg you not to mess up my politics."

Then the English invited the Emperor to the very last
curio-cabinet of all, where they had assembled from all
over the world mineral stones and nymphusorias, starting
with the most enormous of Egyptian keramids and ending with the subcutaneous flea, which is invisible to the
naked eye and bites one between skin and body.

The Emperor drove there.

They viewed the keramids and all the stuffed dummies,
and then came out again, and Platov thinks to himself:

" Thank the Lord, there was nothing there to surprise
the Emperor."

But when they came to the very last chamber, there
before them stood workmen in aprons and working waistcoats, holding a tray. And on the tray there was nothing
at all.

The Emperor was very surprised: why were they presenting an empty tray?

" What does this mean?" he asks; and the English
craftsmen reply:

" This is our humble offering to Your Majesty."

" But what is it?"

" Sire," they say, " do you deign to see this speck of
dust?"

The Emperor looks hard, and sees: on the silver tray
lies the minutest speck of dust.

The workmen say:

" Have the Imperial goodness to spit on your finger

and take the speck of dust in your palm."

"Why should I pick up a speck of dust?"

"This," they reply, "is no speck of dust, but a nymphusoria."

"A live one?"

"By no means," they reply; "it is not living, but made of the purest English steel, and forged by us in the likeness of a flea. And in the centre is a clockwork. Deign to turn the little key, and straightway it will commence to dance all manner of dances."

The Emperor is interested, and asks:

"But where *is* the little key?"

And the Englishmen reply:

"Here too is the key, before your eyes."

"Come," says the Emperor. "No key can I perceive."

"Seeing," they reply, "as how you has to look at it through a microsnoop."

They handed him the microsnoop, and the Emperor saw that by the flea a little key in fact lay on the tray.

"Deign," they say, "to take the flea in your palm. In its little belly there is a hole to wind it up, and you have to turn the key seven times, and then it will start dancing."

With enormous difficulty the Emperor took up the key, scarcely able to hold it between his thumb and first finger, and between the first finger and thumb of the other hand he took the tiny flea, and he had no sooner inserted the key than he felt how it began to wiggle its whiskers; then it began to stir its legs, and all of a sudden it gave a leap, and in the one leap it performed a dance and two furiations to one side and a third furiation to the other side, and thus in three furiations it danced the whole quadrille.

The Emperor at once ordered the Englishmen to be given a million in any currency they chose, whether in silver five-copeck pieces or in small bills.

The English asked for the sum in silver, as they were unfamiliar with paper-money; and then they demonstrated their second stroke of cunning: They were presenting the Emperor with the flea, but had provided no case for it; yet without a case it was impossible to take either flea or key, for they would inevitably go astray and be thrown in the dust-bin. But they happened to have a case that would just fit it, carved from a diamond, with a place scooped out in the middle to hold it. This case they could not give away, alleging that it was Government property, and as regards Government property, even in the case of a visiting Emperor, the regulations were very strict.

At first Platov felt very angry, because, as he said:

"What roguery! They've made a present and pocketed a million, and still it's not enough for them! There's always," said he, "a case to go with such things."

But the Emperor says:

"That'll do, if you don't mind; this is none of your business. Please don't interfere in my policies. These people have their own customs." And he asks: "What is the price of that diamond that has a place in it for the flea?"

The English priced it at a further five thousand.

The Emperor Alexander Pavlovich said: "Pay!" and himself slipped the flea into the hollow diamond, and the key with it, and so as not to lose the diamond he put it into his golden snuff-box, and ordered the snuff-box to be deposited in his small travelling-trunk that was lined with mother-of-pearl and fish-bone. And the English craftsmen he dismissed with great honours, saying to them: "You are the first craftsmen in all the world, and my people can do nothing to compare."

This pleased them very much, and Platov could find nothing to gainsay his Emperor. He just took the micro-snoop and without a word slipped it into his pocket, because, he said to himself, it was all part of the same job, and they had been paid enough as it was.

The Emperor knew nothing of this till they left for

Russia; and this they did soon enough, for the Emperor
had been filled with melancholy by the sight of all these
martial contraptions and desired to unbosom himself to
Fedot the priest in Taganrog. On the journey he and
Platov exchanged very few agreeable words, for their
thoughts were entirely different: the Emperor held that
the English had no peers in art, while Platov affirmed
that if our people were shown anything they could produce something as good or better, but they lacked suitable
instruction. And he represented to the Emperor that the
English had quite different rules of life, science and victu-
alling, and hence had quite a different view of existence.

The Emperor soon wearied of hearing this, and at every
stop on the way Platov would get out and drink in his
vexation a large glass of vodka, chew a salted cracknel,
light his briar pipe, in which there was room for a whole
pound of Zhukov tobacco at once, and then silently resume
his seat at the Emperor's side. The Emperor looked out
of one window, and Platov poked his pipe out at the other
and smoked into the wind. So they reached Petersburg;
but the Emperor did not take Platov with him when he
travelled on to visit Fedot the priest.

" You," he said, " are unrestrained in spiritual discourse,
and you smoke such a lot that from your smoking my head
is full of soot."

Platov was cut to the quick, and going home he lay
down on his grouch-couch and lay there grouching and
smoking Zhukov tobacco without stopping.

Chapter Four

The marvellous flea of burnished English steel remained
with Alexander Pavlovich in the trunk lined with fish-
bone until he passed away in Taganrog, having entrusted
it to Fedot the priest with instructions that he should
deliver it to the Empress when she was out of mourning.
The Empress Elizabeth watched the flea's furiations,
smiled, and then showed no further interest.

" My affair," says she, " is now widowhood, and no amusements have any charm." And returning to Petersburg she put aside the marvel, together with all the other valuables, as a heritage for the successor.

At first the Emperor Nicholas Pavlovich also bestowed no attention on the flea, for there were disturbances at the time of his accession; but one day he began looking through the trunk he had inherited from his brother, and took from it the snuff-box, and from the snuff-box the hollow diamond, and in the diamond he found the steel flea, which had not been wound up for a long time and so was inactive, lying there inoffensively as though putrefied.

The Emperor looked at it, and was amazed.

" What nonsense is this, and why should my brother have preserved it with such care?"

The court servants wanted to throw it into the dust-bin, but the Emperor said :

" No. There must be some point in it."

They summoned the chemist from the shop by the Anichkin Bridge, the one who weighed out poisons on the tiniest of scales, and showed it him; and he at once took the flea, put it on his tongue and said : " I feel coldness, as of firm metal." Then he bit it lightly and declared :

" As you wish, but this is no ordinary flea, it is a nymphusoria, and constructed of metal; and this is not our work, not Russian work."

The Emperor at once ordered inquiries to be made : whence it came and what it signified.

They hastened to examine the acts and records—but found in them no mention of it. They began to interrogate this one and that—but no one knew a thing. By great good fortune the Don Cossack Platov was still alive and was even lying on his grouch-couch puffing away at his pipe. When he heard of the commotion at the palace he at once rose from his couch, threw down his pipe and

appeared before the Emperor wearing all his decorations.
The Emperor says:

"What, martial old man, do you need of me?"

And Platov replies:

"For myself, Your Majesty, I need nothing; I have
enough to eat and drink, and am contented with my lot.
But," says he, "I have come to report in the matter of this
nymphusoria that has been found; this," says he, "was
thus and thus, and that is how it happened before my very
eyes, in England. And there is a key to it, and I have
their microsnoop through which you can see it, and with
the little key you can wind up this here nymphusoria
through the belly and then it will skip about to any extent
you like, and do furiations to one side and the other."

So they wound it up, and about it skipped, and Platov
said:

"This, Your Majesty," he says, "is in truth very fine
and interesting work, but it is not fitting that we should
merely view it with exultation of feeling alone; we should
submit it to Russian scrutiny in Tula or Sesterbek "—in
those days Sestroretsk was still called Sesterbek—" to see
whether our Russian craftsmen cannot excel it, so that
the English shall not judge themselves too exalted above
the Russians."

The Emperor Nicholas Pavlovich had great confidence
in his Russian people and much disliked playing second
fiddle to foreigners, and so he replied to Platov, saying:

"These words of yours, worthy old man, are true
words, and I hereby command that this matter be entrusted to your management. This little box is in any case
of no use to me, immersed as I am in cares; so take it
with you, and lie no more on your grouch-couch, but
travel to the quiet Don and hold internecine converse with
my doughty Don Cossacks concerning their life and their
loyalty and what pleases and displeases them. And
when you are passing through Tula reveal this
nymphusoria to my Tula craftsmen, and let them bend

their minds to it. Tell them from me that my brother
wondered at this strange thing and praised those who
wrought it beyond measure, but that I have faith in my
people and know that they are as good as any. They
will mark my words and do something to justify my
trust."

Chapter Five

Platov took the steel flea, and when he was passing
through Tula he showed it to the Tula armourers and
repeated to them the Emperor's words; and then he asks :

"What are we to do, good people?"

The armourers reply :

"We, granfer, appreciate the Emperor's gracious
words, and will never forget that he puts his trust in his
people; but as to what we are to do in this present case
we are unable to say right off, for the nation of the
English is far from stupid, and even fairly cunning, and
in all arts very artful. To match ourselves with such a
people we must take thought, and invoke God's blessing.
But if you, granfer, trust us as does our Emperor, go
your way to the quiet Don, and leave this flea here with
us, just as it is, in its case in the golden snuff-box. Sojourn
by the Don and heal the wounds you have received in
your country's defence, and when you are returning
through Tula, stop here and send for us; by that time,
God grant, we shall have thought of something."

Platov was somewhat displeased that the men of Tula
required so much time and furthermore did not clearly
reveal what exactly they hoped to contrive. He questioned them this way and that, and in all manners
probed them with true Don shrewdness; but in shrewdness the men of Tula were his match, and they had
conceived a notion concerning which they did not even
think that Platov would believe them, and preferred
first to execute their daring plan and only then to make it
public.

They said:

"We ourselves do not yet know what we shall undertake, and we must simply trust in God, and perhaps the Emperor will have no cause to rue his gracious words."

Thus Platov used his wits and the men of Tula theirs.

Platov twisted and turned, but at last saw that he could in no wise circumscribe the men of Tula, so he gave them the snuff-box containing the nymphusoria and said:

"Very well," says he, "let it be as you wish; I know the men you are, but there's no help for it; I'll trust you, but see that you do not substitute the diamond or mar the delicate English work; and do your work speedily, for I travel fast: ere two weeks have elapsed I shall turn back from the quiet Don on my way to Petersburg, and then there must without fail be something for me to show the Emperor."

The armourers set his mind at rest:

"We will not harm the fine work, neither will we substitute the diamond; and the space of two weeks will suffice, and when you turn back there will be something worthy of placing before His Imperial Majesty."

But as to *what exactly* it would be they said not a word.

Chapter Six

Platov drove away from Tula, and three of the armourers, the cunningest of all—one of them being a left-handed man with a squint in his eye, a birthmark on his cheek and all the hair on his temples torn out in his apprentice days—bade adieu to their fellows and their families and without telling anyone where they were going took their knapsacks, packed them with the victuals they needed and departed from the town.

All that was observed was that they went not through the Moscow Gate but in the opposite direction, along the Kiev road; and people thought that they must be going to Kiev to pay their respects to the sacred relics, or to take counsel with one or other of the holy men still of this world of whom there is always an abundance in Kiev.

But this was only close to the truth, but not the truth itself. Neither time nor distance permitted the Tula craftsmen to make their way to Kiev on foot in the space of three weeks and then have leisure to devise something to bring shame upon the nation of the English. More easily could they have gone to say their prayers in Moscow, which lay only twice ninety versts away, and where there is abundance of the relics of holy men. Whereas in the opposite direction it was also twice ninety versts to Orel, and from Orel to Kiev at least another five hundred. Such a journey is not easily to be made, and when it is made one cannot easily recover from it: long will the legs be numb and the hands a-tremble.

Some folk even thought that the craftsmen had boasted wildly to Platov and then, when they came to their senses, their courage had failed them and they had run away, taking with them the Emperor's gold snuff-box, and the hollow diamond, and the flea of English steel that had caused them so much concern.

But this supposition was completely unfounded, and unworthy of the skilful men in whom the hopes of the nation now resided.

Chapter Seven

The men of Tula, clever folk and well-versed in the art of working metal, are also well-known for their great knowledge of religion. Their native land is full of their fame in this respect, and Mount Athos too: they are not only great ones for singing complicated part-songs, but also know how to copy the picture of the Angelus; and such as consecrate themselves to a higher service and don the monkish gown gain further fame as the best men for running monasteries and collecting alms. On Mount Athos it is known that the people of Tula are profitable folk, and that but for them the dark corners of the Russian land would certainly not see many a sacred relic from

the remote East, and Mount Athos itself would be deprived
of much useful tribute from Russian lavishness and piety.

Nowadays "the Tula men of Athos" trade holy relics
over all our Russian land, and are experts at gathering
collections even from such places as have nothing to give.
The men of Tula are full of ecclesiastical ardour and dili-
gent in their religious practices, and so the three craftsmen who had undertaken to support Platov, and with
him the whole of Russia, made no mistake when they
turned their steps not towards Moscow but southwards.
They did not go to Kiev, however, but to Mtsensk, a town
in the Government of Orel in which there is to be found
the ancient ikon of St. Nicholas, hewn from stone, which
floated thither down the river Zusha many centuries ago,
borne on a stone cross. This icon is of a dread and terrify-
ing appearance; on it the saint is represented full-length,
clad in a garment of silver-gilt, sombre of face and bearing
in one hand a temple and in the other a sword. And in
this sword is the sense of the thing: for St. Nicholas is
the patron saint of mercantile and military matters, and
the Nicholas of Mtsensk in particular; and it was to him
that the craftsmen from Tula went to pay their respects.
They held a service before the icon, another by the stone
cross; then returned home in the dead of night and saying
no word to anyone began their work in the greatest of
secrecy. All three gathered in the house of the left-handed
artisan, fastened the doors, closed the shutters, lit the
lamp before the picture of St. Nicholas and set about their
task.

One day, two, three they sit there, never stirring abroad,
tapping away with their little hammers. They are forging something, but what they are forging no one knows.

Everyone is curious, but no one can find out anything
at all, because those at work say not a word and never
appear outside the house. Various people came to the
house, knocked at the door under different pretexts, asking
for a light or some salt, but the three craftsmen opened

to no knock, and it was even not known what they were existing on. People tried to scare them out, pretending that the house next door was on fire, hoping that they might run out in terror and reveal what it was they had forged; but nothing could diddle those cunning artisans: once only did the left-handed smith poke his shoulders through the window and cry:

"Let it burn; we have no time for such things!" and then he drew in his close-plucked head, slammed the shutter and resumed his labours.

All that was visible through the little chinks was a fire glowing inside the house, and all that could be heard was the little hammers rapping away on the loud-sounding anvils.

In a word, everything was done in such absolute secrecy that nothing at all could be discovered; and this went on till the Cossack Platov arrived once more on his way from the quiet Don to the Emperor, and all this time the craftsmen saw no one and spoke to no one.

Chapter Eight

Platov travelled fast, and ceremoniously: he himself sat in his open carriage, and on the box sat two Cossack disorderlies, one on either side of the driver, with whips in their hands, lashing the driver mercilessly to keep him up to scratch. And if either of the Cossacks dozed off in his seat Platov would lift his boot and give him a kick, and off they would dash even more furiously than before. These measures of encouragement were so efficacious that at no stopping-place was it possible to rein in the horses at once, and the speed of their motion always carried them a hundred paces beyond the appointed place. Then the Cossacks would undertake retroactive measures on the driver, and they would drive back to the stopping-place.

So they came galloping to Tula, and dashed a hundred paces beyond the Moscow Gate, and then the Cossacks acted with their whips on the driver in the reverse direc-

tion, and at the porch they began to harness fresh horses.
Platov did not get down from the carriage, but ordered
one of the Cossacks to fetch without delay the artisans
with whom he had left the flea.

One Cossack ran off to tell them to come with all speed,
bringing the work with which they were to shame the
English; and not content with this, Platov sent speeding
after him more disorderlies and still more, to ensure that
they should come without delay.

When he had dispatched all his Cossacks he even began
to send off simple folk from among the curious public,
and in his impatience started to put his legs out of the carriage, anxious to run off himself, and ground his teeth—
they seemed to be taking such a time.

In those days everything was required to be executed
with the utmost dispatch, so that not a moment should be
wasted that might contribute to the well-being of Russia.

Chapter Nine

The Tula craftsman who had executed the remarkable
undertaking were at this moment only just completing
their task. The Cossacks dashed up to them all out of
breath, and the simple folk from the curious public didn't
get there at all, for, being unaccustomed to hurrying, their
legs went all to pieces on the road, and then in fear of
meeting Platov again they made off home and hid themselves as best they could.

But no sooner had the Cossacks reached the house than
they let out a shattering shout, and when they saw that
the door was not opened to them, without beating about
the bush they began to tug at the bolts on the shutters;
but the bolts were so solid that they yielded not an inch.
Then they battered at the door, but the door was fastened
inside with an oaken bar. So the Cossacks took a beam
from the street, propped the beam under the eaves in the
way firemen do, and with one short heave levered the roof
off the little house. But no sooner had they got the roof

off than they fell over backwards, because in the little
chamber where the craftsmen were working there had
gathered from their unceasing labours such a frousty fug
that anyone from the fresh air simply had his breath taken
away.

The emissaries cried :

" What are you, you so-and-so's, you scoundrels, up to,
that you even dare to knock us sideways with this frousty
fug? Have you no fear of God? "

And the craftsmen replied :

" We'll be ready in a moment; we're just hammering
the last nail home, and when we've hammered it home
we'll bring our work out."

But the emissaries said :

" Before that happens he'll have eaten us alive, leaving
nothing to hold a funeral service over ! "

And the craftsmen responded :

" He won't want to swallow you, for while you have
been talking the last nail has been driven home. Run
and tell him that we are bringing our work forthwith."

The Cossacks ran off, but not at all convinced; they
thought the craftsmen were deceiving them.   So they
kept glancing back; but the craftsmen were coming along
behind them, and even hurrying, so that they were not
even correctly attired to appear before an important per-
sonage, and were hooking the hooks of their kaftans as
they ran. Two of them were carrying nothing at all in
their hands, and the third, the left-handed one, bore in
a green canvas case the Emperor's travelling-trunk with
the English steel flea inside.

Chapter Ten

The Cossacks ran up to Platov and said :

" Here they are in person ! "

And Platov said to the craftsmen :

" Finished?"

" It's all," they replied, " finished and done."

I

" Hand it over."

They handed it over.

And the carriage was already harnessed and the driver and postillion in their places. The disorderlies took their seats on either side of the driver and raised their whips over him, and held them there, menacingly.

Platov tore off the green canvas, opened the trunk, took the golden snuff-box out of its wrapping of cotton wool, and out of the snuff box the hollow diamond, and he saw: the English flea lay as it had lain before, and apart from it there was nothing at all.

Platov said :

" What's the meaning of this? Where is the work that was to gladden the heart of the Emperor?"

But the armourers replied :

" Here it is, our work."

Platov asked :

" Then what is it?"

But the armourers replied :

" What is there to explain? Here it is, all before your eyes. Just take a good look."

Platov shrugged his shoulders, crying :

" Where is the key to the flea?"

" Right here," they replied. " Where the flea is, there is the key, all in the same hollow diamond."

Platov wished to pick up the key, but his fingers were stubby; he kept fumbling and fumbling, but could get a hold neither of the flea nor of the key that wound it up through the hole in the belly; and suddenly he lost his temper and began to use coarse words as Cossacks do.

He cried :

" So, you scoundrels, you've done nothing at all, and into the bargain, I'll be bound, ruined the whole ruddy issue ! I'll have your heads for this!"

But the men of Tula, in reply :

" Wrongly you revile us so. From you, as from the representative of the Emperor, it is our bounden duty to suffer all manner of abuse; but because you have doubted us, even believing us capable of taking the Emperor's name in vain, we will not now reveal to you the secret of our work. Do you convey it to the Emperor, and he shall see the sort of people he has, and whether he need feel ashamed of them."

And Platov cried:

"You're lying, you rogues, and we shan't part like this; one of you shall travel with me to Petersburg, and there I will put him to the test, to get to the bottom of your cunning."

And with these words he thrust out his hand, seized in his stubby fingers the collar of the left-handed craftsman with a squint, so that all the hooks in his kaftan flew out, and threw him at his feet on the carriage floor.

"Sit there," he said, "like a pooble-dog till we get to Petersburg; you shall answer for the three. And you," he said to the Cossacks, "get to it! No slackness: I must be with the Emperor in Petersburg the day after to-morrow."

All that the artisans could pluck up courage to ask concerning their fellow was how Platov dare carry him off without a duckament. For without a duckament he wouldn't be able to come back. But in reply Platov showed them his fist, such a fearsome fist—all gnarled and cut to pieces and healed up again in horrifying scars—and threatened them, saying: "Here's your duckament!" And to the Cossacks he said:

"Off we go!"

The Cossacks, the driver and the horses all started work at once, and off they shot with the left-handed artisan and without a duckament; and in a day, as Platov had ordered, they swept up to the Emperor's palace and even, as usual, shot past the marble columns of the entrance.

Platov stood up, pinned on his decorations and went to see the Emperor, leaving the left-handed artisan under the guard of the Cossacks at the porch.

Chapter Eleven

Platov feared to appear before the Emperor, for
Nicholas Pavlovich was terribly observant, and he had an
extraordinary memory and never forgot a thing. Platov
knew that he would without fail be asked about the flea.
And he, who feared no foe in all the world, felt his heart
sink into his boots : he went into the palace with the little
trunk, and quietly slipped it behind the stove in the parlour.   When he had hidden it he appeared before the
Emperor in his study and began to report the internecine
conversations he had had with the Cossacks on the quiet
Don. What he thought was that he must interest the
Emperor in this, and if the Emperor himself remembered
and began to speak of the flea he would have to hand it
over and tell him all about it, but if not, not; he would tell
the Emperor's valet to hide the little trunk, and he would
throw the left-handed artisan into a dungeon and keep
him sitting there indefinitely, till such time as he might
be required.

But the Emperor Nicholas Pavlovich forgot never a
thing, and hardly had Platov finished his account of the
internecine conversations on the Don than he up and
asked him :

" Well, and how have my Tula craftsmen shown their
mettle in the matter of the English nymphusoria?"

Platov replied as the matter appeared to him.

" The nymphusoria, Your Majesty," he said, " is of the
same dimensions as before, and I have brought it back;
but the men of Tula could do nothing to counter it.'

The Emperor replied :

" You are a worthy old man, but what you are now
telling me cannot correspond to the facts."

Platov tried to convince him, relating all that had hap-
pened; and when he came to the point where the men of
Tula had asked him to show the flea to the Emperor,
Nicholas Pavlovich patted him on the shoulder and said :

" Go and fetch it. I know that my people will never let
me down. There's more in this than meets the eye."

Chapter Twelve

The trunk was fetched from behind the stove and the
canvas cover removed; they opened the golden snuff-box
and took out the hollow diamond, and there lay the flea
as it had lain before.

The Emperor looked, and said:

" What the deuce!" But his faith in his Russian craftsmen did not diminish, and he ordered them to summon
his favourite daughter Alexandra Nikolayevna, and when
she came running he said to her:

" My daughter, thy fingers are slender; take up the little
key and make haste to wind this nymphusoria's abomin-
able mechanism."

The Princess began to turn the key, and straightway
the flea waggled its whiskers, but never a stir from its feet.
Alexandra Nikolayevna wound up the clockwork as far
as it would go, but the nymphusoria refused to dance a
step and to perform any one of the furiations it had
whilom performed.

Platov turned green in the face, and cried:

" Ha, the currish rascals! Now I understand why they
wouldn't tell me a thing. It's lucky that I brought one
of the fools with me."

With these words he ran out to the entrance, seized the
left-handed artisan by the hair and began to jerk him this
way and that, so that his hair flew out in lumps. But
when Platov had finished mauling him the artisan
straightened himself up and said:

" As it was, all my hair was torn out in my apprentice
days, and I know not why it was necessary to repeat the
operation."

" It was because I put my trust in you," said Platov,
"and vouched for you; and now you have ruined a rarity."

The left-handed artisan replied:

" We are very pleased that you should have vouched for us; but as for ruining, we have ruined nothing; take it and look at it through the most powerful microsnoop you have."

Platov hurried off and told them to fetch the microsnoop, but the left-handed artisan he threatened:

" As for you, you so-and-so," said he, " I'll so-and-so you in a way you won't forget!"

And he ordered the Cossacks to twist the artisan's arms behind his back more sternly than before, and himself climbed the steps, panting and saying a prayer to himself: " Blessed Mother of the Blessed King," and so on and so forth. But the courtiers who were standing on the steps all turned away from him, thinking: Platov has cooked his goose, and now he will be driven in shame from the Imperial presence. They couldn't bear him, he was so brave.

Chapter Thirteen

When Platov reported to the Emperor the words of the left-handed artisan, at once his Majesty said cheerfully:

" I knew that my Russians would not let me down." And he ordered them to serve him the microsnoop on a silk cushion.

Straightway the microsnoop was produced, and the Emperor took the flea and placed it beneath the glass first back upwards, then sideways, then on its belly; turned it, in a word, in every direction, but nothing was to be seen. But even now the Emperor did not lose faith; he simply said:

" Fetch me that armourer who is below."

Platov reported:

" He ought to be tittivated up a bit. He was taken as he stood, and now he looks rather the worse for wear."

But the Emperor replied:

" Never mind. Bring him in as he is."

Platov said to the artisan:

" Now you go in there, you so-and-so, and answer to

the Emperor in person."

And the artisan replied :

" Right. I will go and I will answer."

He went in as he was : his feet wrapped up in rags, one trouser-leg in his boot and other flapping, his kaftan ever so old, with hooks that wouldn't fasten, some of them missing, and his collar torn.

" What of it?" he thought to himself. " If the Emperor desires to see me I must appear before him; and that I have no duckament with me is not my fault, and I will tell him how things befell."

When the artisan entered and bowed, the Emperor at once addressed him :

" What is the meaning of this, brother, that we have scrutinized it in this way and that, and peered at it through the microsnoop, and yet cannot perceive anything to surprise or amaze us?"

And the artisan replied :

" Did Your Majesty take a proper look?"

The magnates shook their heads at him to indicate that he should not address His Imperial Majesty in that way; but he didn't understand the courtiers' way of speaking with flattery or cunning, and so he spoke simply.

The Emperor said :

" Stop bothering him; let him answer as best he can."

And at once he explained to the artisan :

" We," he said, " put it this way." And he placed the flea beneath the microsnoop. " Look for yourself," he said; " there's nothing to be seen."

The artisan replied :

" In this way, Your Majesty, nothing can be seen, for our work is infinitely more secretive compared with those dimensions."

The Emperor asked :

" Then how must one look?"

" It is necessary," said the artisan, " to bring one of the feet in detail beneath the microsnoop and look separately at the heel."

"Goodness gracious!" said the Emperor. "That will require very close peering."

"It can't be helped," replied the artisan, "seeing as that's the only way in which our work can be perceived; and if you do so our surprise will become manifest."

They placed the flea as the left-handed smith had indicated, and no sooner had the emperor looked through the upper glass than he beamed all over his Imperial face. He took hold of the artisan, just as he was, dishevelled and unwashed and covered with dust, and embraced him and kissed him, and then he turned to his courtiers and said:

"You see, I know better than anyone that my Russians would not let me down. Just take a look: the rascals have taken the English flea and shod its hoofs!"

Chapter Fourteen

They all drew near and looked, and they saw that the flea had in fact a real shoe on every hoof. But the artisan declared that this was not the end of the surprise.

"If the microsnoop were more powerful," he said, "and could magnify five million times, you would see," said he, "that on each hoof the craftsman's name is inscribed: which Russian artisan made which hoof."

"And is your name here?" asked the Emperor.

"By no means," replied the artisan. "My name is missing."

"Why so?"

"Because," said he, "the work I did was tinier even than these shoes; I forged the nails with which they were put on; and that's something that no microsnoop you ever saw could render visible."

The Emperor asked:

"Then what microsnoop did you use to perform this wonder?"

And the left-handed smith replied:

" We are poor people, and our poverty permits us no microsnoops; we just have to squint in a certain way."

And now the courtiers, seeing what a success the artisan was, began to embrace him, and Platov gave him a hundred roubles and said:

" Forgive me, brother, for tearing out your hair."

The artisan replied:

" God will forgive you. 'Tis not the first time we've been so bald."

And he said not another word; nor was there time, for the Emperor ordered the shod nymphusoria to be packed up and sent back to England, as a gift, so that they should understand that they had not succeeded in surprising us. And the Emperor ordered that the flea should be conveyed there by a special courier speaking all languages; and the artisan was to go with him, so that he himself might show the English the work that had been done and the sort of artisans they had in Tula.

Platov gave him his blessing.

" God bless you," he said; " and for the journey I will send you some of my own special vodka. Don't drink little, don't drink much ; just drink a nice medium quantity."

And he kept his word, and sent along a few bottles.

And Count Nettlerod ordered the smith to be washed all over at the Tulyakov popular baths, have his hair cut at a barber's and be clad in the Sunday kaftan of a court singer, so that it might appear that he was invested with some sort of salaried rank.

When they had thus decked him out they gave him a drink of tea laced with Platov's special vodka, tied his belt at tight as possible, so that his inside should not be jolted about, and conveyed him to London. And so began his experiences in foreign parts.

Chapter Fifteen

The courier and the artisan travelled fast, not stopping

for a rest anywhere between Petersburg and London; but at each post-house they tightened their belts another inch, so that their guts should not get mixed up with their lungs; and as the artisan, after being presented to the Emperor, had on Platov's order been given a free run of the Government liquor-stores, without eating a bite he maintained himself on what he had been able to collect, and sang Russian songs to the whole of Europe, adding however a foreign refrain: "*Aïe louli, c'est très jouli.*"

When the courier had brought him to London he explained to whom it concerned what it was all about, and handed over the Emperor's travelling-trunk, and he found a room for the artisan at an hotel; but here the smith soon began to feel bored, and also peckish. He knocked on a door and indicated his mouth to one of the menials, and the latter led him forthwith to the restarong.

Here the smith took a seat at a table, and there he sat, but as for saying something in English, he simply couldn't. But he soon had an idea, and simply tapped on the table with his finger and pointed to his mouth; the English cottoned on right away and served him with food, though not always with the right dishes, but such as, being unacceptable to him, he could not accept. They served him after their fashion with a pudding all on fire, and he said, I don't know about eating a thing like that; nor did he. So they took it away and brought something else. Nor would he touch their vodka, for it is green, as though laced with vitriol; but chose the most natural of beverages and sat over his bottle of vodka in the cool waiting for the courier.

But the personages to whom the courier had handed the nymphusoria at once examined it under their most powerful microsnoop, and straightway prepared a prescription of it for publication in the press.

"And this same craftsman," said they, "we should like to see without delay."

The courier conducted them to the hotel and thence to

the restarong, where they found the artisan with a happy
smile on his face and a deep blush on his nose; and the
courier said : " There he is."

The Englishman at once clapped the artisan on the
shoulder and took him by the hand as though he were
their equal; "Kamerad," they said, "good kamerad, good
workman; we'll have a good long talk with you later on,
but first of all we must drink your health."

They called for a lot to drink and handed the artisan
the first glass, but he, being a polite fellow, didn't like to
drink before the others; he thought that in their mortifi-
cation they might try to poison him.

" No," he said, " I can't forget that I'm simply a guest
here; you go ahead and drink first."

The Englishmen tasted all the wines before him and
then poured him out a glass. He stood up, crossed himself
with his left hand and drank the health of one and all.

They noticed that he crossed himself with his left hand,
and asked the courier :

" What is he, a Lutheran or a Protestantist?"

The courier replied :

" He is neither Lutheran nor Protestantist, but of the
Russian faith."

" But why does he cross himself with his left hand?"

The courier said :

"Being left-handed, he does everything with his left
hand."

The Englishmen were more surprised than ever, and
began to pump wine into the artisan and the courier, and
this went on for three days; and then they said : " This
must suffice for the moment." Each swallowed a sym-
phon of soddy-water; then, quite themselves again, they
began questioning the smith : where he had studied, and
what, and which page he had reached in the arithmetic
book.

The artisan replied :

" Our studies are very simple : the Psalm-Book, and the

Dream-Book, and arithmetic not at all."

The English glanced at one another, and said :

" Amazing !"

And the artisan went on :

" So it is with us all."

" And what," they asked, " might the Dream-Book be?"

" This," said he, " is such a book, that if in the Psalm-Book King David did not clearly reveal something concerning dreams, then in the Dream-Book you can find a satisfactory exposition."

They said :

" Pitiful ! It would be better if of arithmetic you at least knew the four rules of addition; this would profit you more than all the Dream-Books in the world. Then you would be able to calculate the extent of the power in each and every mechanism; as it is, you are indeed skilful with your hands, but you were unable to reckon that so tiny a mechanism as this nymphusoria is exact to the last fraction of an inch, and that the addition of shoes will throw the whole thing out of balance. Hence it comes that the nymphusoria leaps no longer, neither does it dance the quadrille."

The artisan agreed.

" There's no disputing," said he, " that we're rather unscientific in our science; but we're nonetheless devoted to our fatherland."

And the Englishmen said to him :

" Stay here with us; we'll give you a good education and make a marvellous craftsman of you."

But to this the artisan wouldn't agree.

" At home," said he, " are my old parents."

The Englishmen offered to send his parents money, but the artisan wouldn't accept.

" We," said he " are attached to our homeland, and my father is an old man and my mother an old woman and accustomed to go to church in her own parish; and as for me I should feel very lonely here, for I am as yet unmarried."

"You," they told him, "will grow accustomed to our ways; you'll adopt our faith, and we'll find a wife for you."

"This," said the smith, "can never be."

"Why not?"

"Because," he replied, "our Russian faith is the true faith, and as our forefathers believed so must their prodigies."

"But you," said the Englishmen, "are not familiar with our faith. We hold to the same Christian law and read the same Gospel."

"The Gospel is in truth," said he, "the same for all; but our books are thicker than your books, and our faith fuller."

"How can you judge that?"

"Since in our lands," he replied, "there are visible proofs on every hand."

"How so?"

"Such proofs," said he, "as traumaturgic icons, and skulls that sweat blood, and sacred relics; whereas you have nothing, and even, save for the Sabbath, no holidays. And the second reason is that even if I were to marry her according to the law, it would be embarrassing for me to live with an Englishwoman."

"Why?" they asked. "Don't look down your nose at our women; they too dress neatly, and are good house-wives."

But the smith replied:

"I know them not."

The Englishman said:

"Fiddle-faddle. That can easily be aranged; we'll fix you up a grandez-vous."

The smith felt embarrassed.

"Why," he said, "worry the girls for nothing?" And he turned the proposal down. "A grandez-vous," he

said, " is a matter for gentlemen, and becomes us not, and
if they learnt about it at home in Tula I'd never hear the
end of it."

The English were curious.

" But if you have no grandez-vouses, how do you
arrange to make a satisfactory choice? "

The smith explained how things are with us.

" In our country," he said, " if a man desires to reveal
a circumstantial intention with regard to a girl, he sends
an eloquent match-maker, and when the woman has
made a proposal they go decently to the girl's house and
scan her openly in the presence of all her kith and kin."

They understood him, but replied that there were no
match-makers in England nor were such customs current,
and the smith said :

" This is all the more acceptable, since if one would
occupy oneself with such things it should be with a circumstantial intention, and as I can feel no such thing
towards an alien nation, why delude the girls? "

With these words too he pleased the English, so that
they once more began slapping him amiably on the back
and on the knees, and asked :

" All," they said, " that we should like to know is what
flaws you have observed in our girls, and why you avoid
them."

And the smith replied frankly :

" I find no flaws in them, and all that displeases me is
that their garments seem to float around, and you can't
make out what they have put on, or why; on top there's
something, and then something else pinned on below, and
on their arms some sort of leggings. Dolled up like so
many Jackanapeses."

The English laughed, and said :

" Why should their clothes be a hindrance to you?"

" A hindrance, no," replied the smith; " I'm simply
afraid that I should be ashamed to watch while she dis-
entangled herself from all that."

" You really consider your fashions preferable?"

" The fashions we have in Tula," said he, " are simple : each one wears her own lace; and our lace is such that even great ladies don't scorn it."

They also showed him to their ladies, and tea was poured for him and he was asked :

" Why are you frowning?"

He replied :

" We, you see, are not accustomed to drink it so sweet."

So they gave him a lump to nibble in the Russian way.

They demonstrated that this method is not so satisfactory, but he says :

" To our taste this is tastier."

Nothing the English did could disconcert him or make him take a fancy for their way of life, and they could only persuade him to stay for a short while, promising that during this time they would take him to all sorts of factories and show him the whole of their art.

" And then," said they, " we'll put you on one of our ships and deliver you safe and sound in Petersburg."

To this he agreed.

Chapter Sixteen

The Englishmen took charge of the left-handed smith, and sent the Russian courier back to Russia. Although the courier had a rank, and was learned in all sorts of languages, they weren't interested in him; but they were interested in the left-handed smith, and so they up and started taking him about places and showing him everything. He examined the whole of their production and their metal factories and soap-sawing works, and all their arrangements pleased him greatly, in particular the condition of the workers. Every worker of theirs was constantly well-fed, and clothed not in rags, but each of them had a good stout waistcoat and thick boots with iron blakeys so that his feet should always be comfortable; they worked not by trial and error but after a thorough training, and had a good notion of how things were. Before the eyes of each hung a muchiplication-table, and at his side was a slate; all the time a craftsman was doing something he would keep looking at the muchiplication-table and checking up, and then he would write one thing down on the slate and rub out something else and make it all tot up neatly, and what was down in the figures that too came out in the facts. And when it was Sunday they would gather in pairs, each would take a walking-stick in his hand and they would walk out and amuse themselves in a decent and respectable way.

The smith had a good look at all their life and all their works; but most attention of all he devoted to such an object that the English were quite surprised. He wasn't so interested in the way they made new guns as in the condition of the old ones. He would go around praising everything, and say:

" We can do the same."

But as soon as he caught sight of an old gun he would poke his finger into the muzzle, pass his hand over the barrel and sigh:

" This," he would say, " is incomprehensively more comprehensive than anything we can do."

The English simply couldn't imagine what he was getting at, and he would ask:

" Would it be possible for me to know whether our generals ever saw this?"

They replied:

" Such as came here must have."

" And what sort of generals were they?" he asked. " With gloves or without?"

" Your generals," said they, " are parade-generals; they are never without gloves, and so they must have had them here."

The smith said nothing. But suddenly he began to pine. He pined and pined, and said to the Englishmen:

" Thank you very much for all your hospitality; I'm

very pleased with everything I've seen, and everything I needed to see I have seen, and now I should like to go home."

And they couldn't keep him any longer. They wouldn't let him go by land, for he couldn't speak all languages, but neither did a sea-voyage seem a good idea, for it was autumn and the weather stormy. But he insisted : Please let me go now.

"We have looked at the stormometer," they said, "and it says there's going to be a storm. You may be drowned; you know, this isn't the Gulf of Finland, but the Murderitanean Sea itself."

"It's all the same," said he, "where one dies; it's all in the hand of God, and I wish to return without delay to my native place, for otherwise I am liable to be beset by a sort of lunacy."

They couldn't keep him there by force, so they gave him a good blow-out, and some money, and as a souvenir a gold watch with a musical inside, and to protect him from the chill of the sea on his late autumn journey they gave him a baize overcoat with a hood for his head. They dressed him warmly and brought him to a ship that was sailing for Russia. Here they settled him in a good berth like a real gentleman, but he didn't like sitting under cover with the other gentlemen, felt ashamed like, and so he would go up on deck, sit down under a tarpaulin, and ask :

"Which way lies Russia?"

The Englishman he had asked would point in some direction, or nod his head that way, and he would turn his face thither and gaze impatiently towards his native land.

As they left the bay and came out into the Murderitanean Sea, his yearning for Russia became so overpowering that it was simply impossible to assuage it. The waves were something awful, but he absolutely refused to go below; he'd sit under the tarpaulin, pull his hood over his brows and gaze towards his homeland.

Many times the English came to him, calling him down to the warmth below, but he, so that they should cease molesting him, even began to tell fibs.

" No," he would say, " I feel better up here on the roof; if I went downstairs the pitching and tossing would pitch and toss my belly about more than I could stand."

And so for the time being he stayed up above, and in this way greatly pleased a certain English kipper who unfortunately for the smith could talk Russian. This kipper couldn't get over his surprise that a land-lugger like the Russian could stand such weather.

" Johnny Roosky, you're a stout lad," he would say. " Let's have a drink."

The Russian had a drink.

And the kipper said :

" Another one !"

And the smith had another one, and then another, and got quite merry.

And the kipper asked him :

" What secret are you conveying from our land to Russia?"

The smith replied :

" That's my business."

" Then," said the kipper, " let us two lay a wager."

" What wager?" asked the smith.

" Why, let neither of us drink by himself, and each drink exactly what the other does, and as much, and we'll see who gets tight first."

The smith thought to himself : the sky's getting dark, and my belly's beginning to bark, and the journey's long and I can't see my homeland because of all the water; it would certainly be more cheerful if we laid a wager.

" Good," he said. " Let's lay the wager."

" Only honest, mind !"

" As for that, don't you worry ! "

And so they agreed and clasped hands on the bargain.

Chapter Seventeen

They laid their wager while they still sailing the Murderitanean Sea, and they went on drinking all the way to Riga, keeping step with one another and never a step behind; and so accurately did they do this that if one, glancing at the waves, saw a devil emerging from the deep, the other never failed to see it either. Only the devil the kipper saw had red hair, whereas the smith asserted that it was a very blackamoor.

The smith said:

" Cross yourself and turn away; here comes a devil out of the sea."

But the Englishman would dispute with him.

" That's no devil, I tell you; it's a deep-sea diver. If you like I'll throw you into the sea, and you'll see that he'll hand you back to me as nice as anything."

And the smith said:

" Throw me, then."

So the kipper took him pick-a-back and carried him to the side.

Some sailors who had seen this stopped him and reported to the captain, and the captain ordered them to be put in irons and given rum and wine and cold food, so that they could drink and eat and carry on with their wager; but they weren't to be served with the pudding all on fire, as that might set light to the spirits inside them.

And so they were brought in irons to Petersburg and neither had won the wager, and here they were put in separate conveyances and the Englishman was taken to the Ambassador's house on the English Quay and the smith was taken to the police-station.

And from then on their fates began to differ considerably.

Chapter Eighteen

When the Englishman was brought to the Ambassador's house they at once called a doctor and a pharmacist, and the doctor ordered him to be placed in a warm bath and the pharmacist rolled a guttapercha pill and popped it into his mouth, and then the two of them took him and placed him on a feather-bed and covered him up with a fur coat and left him there to sweat it out; and so that he shouldn't be disturbed everyone in the Embassy received strict orders not to sneeze. The doctor and the pharmacist waited till the kipper had gone to sleep, and then they prepared him another guttapercha pill, placed it on the table by his bedside and went away.

But the smith was dumped on the floor of the police-station, and questioned:

"Who are you and where do you come from, and have you a passport or any other duckament?"

And he, from his sea-sickness, his drinking and all the pitching and tossing had grown so weak that he couldn't answer a word, but just groaned.

Then they searched him, took off all his clothes, took away the watch with the musical inside and all his money, and the inspector ordered him to be conveyed to the hospital free of charge by the first cab that passed.

A policeman led the smith outside to put him in a cab, but for a long time he couldn't catch one, for cabbies run when they see coppers. And all this time the smith lay on the cold cobbles; and then the policeman caught a cabby, but there wasn't a warm rug in the cab to cover him up with, because on such occasions cabbies conceal their rugs beneath them so that the policemen's feet shall get cold all the quicker. And so the smith was driven along all uncovered, and when they were moving him from one cab to another they kept dropping him, and when they picked him up they would tug him by the ears to bring him to his senses. When they got to the hospital the hospital wouldn't accept him without a duckament, so they took him to another hospital, and they wouldn't accept him there either; and so on to a third and fourth; all night long they drove him all over the town, shifting him from one cab to another, so that he was knocked black and blue. Then at length an assistant doctor told the policeman to take him to the Obukhvin Hospital for Paupers, where they let all the unknowns die.

Here they wanted a receipt, and till this was settled they let the smith lie in the corridor.

And the next morning the English kipper got up, swallowed the other guttapercha pill, had a light breakfast of roast chicken, drank some soddy-water and said:

"Where's my Russian kamerad? I must look for him."

He put on his clothes and hurried out.

Chapter Nineteen

Strange to say, the kipper soon discovered the smith, but they hadn't yet put him to bed and he was still lying on the floor in the corridor. And he complained to the Englishman.

"I," he said, "must without delay have a word with the Emperor."

The Englishman hurried off to Count Kleinmichel and kicked up a fuss:

"How are such things possible? He," said the Englishman, "may wear a sheep's skin, but he has a human soul."

For this observation the Englishman was at once thrown out; he mustn't dare mention the human soul in respectable company. And then someone said to him: "What you ought to do is to go and see the Cossack Platov; he's a man you can talk to." The Englishman visited Platov, who was now once more lying on his grouch-couch. Platov heard what he had to say, and remembered the left-handed smith.

"Of course, brother," he said; "I know him well—even pulled his hair out. But I just don't know how to help him in this mischance; for I retired long ago, and no one respects me any longer. What you had better do is go and see Commander Skobelev; he's a powerful man, and experienced in matters of this sort; he'll be able to do something."

The kipper went to see Skobelev and told him the whole story: what the smith was suffering from, and why. Skobelev said:

"I understand this sickness, but German doctors are unable to cure it, and in such cases you need a practitioner with an ecclesiastical background; for they grow up in such surroundings and know what to do. I'll at once send over the Russian doctor Martyn-Solsky."

But when Martyn-Solsky got there the smith was already passing away, because he had banged the back of his head against the kerbstone, and all he could say distinctly was:

"Tell the Emperor that the English do not clean their guns with crushed brick; let us not do so either, or if——God forfend!—it comes to war our guns will be good for nothing."

And after making this trusty declaration the smith crossed himself and died.

Martyn-Solsky immediately went and reported to Count Chernyshev, and asked to be admitted to the Emperor's presence; and Count Chernyshev yelled at him:

"Keep your mind," said he, "on your emetics and your purges, and don't poke your nose in other people's business: in Russia we have generals to do that."

And so the Emperor was not told, and they went on cleaning their guns with crushed brick right up to the Crimean War. And then, when they loaded their guns, the bullets joggled about, because the barrels were all worn away with the brick. Then Martyn-Solsky reminded Count Chernyshev of the left-handed smith, and Count Chernyshev said:

"Go to the devil, you sawbones; don't interfere in other people's concerns; and if you say anything I'll swear you never breathed a word about it to me, and then you'll catch it."

Martyn-Solsky thought to himself: And so he will, and so I shall. And so he said nothing.

But had he been able to convey to the Emperor the words of the left-handed smith, the Crimean War might have had quite a different ending.

Chapter Twenty

Now all this is a thing of the past, and belongs among the traditions of olden days—though not so olden at that, and one shouldn't be in too much of a hurry to forget such traditions, for all the fabulous cast of our tale and the epic character of its hero. The name of the left-handed smith, like the names of so many of the greatest geniuses, is lost to posterity; but as a myth personified by the popular fancy he is of interest, and his adventures may serve to recall an epoch the spirit of which they truly and accurately reflect.

Craftsmen like the fabulous left-handed smith of course no longer exist in Tula; machines have levelled up the inequality of talent and gifts, and genius can no longer battle with application and accuracy. Fostering the increase of earnings, machines do not foster an artistic boldness which sometimes went too far, inspiring the popular fancy to compose fantastic legends like the present.

The workers can of course appreciate the benefits accruing to them from the practical application of mechanical science, but for all that they recall the days of old with pride and affection. It constitutes their epic, and is anything but lacking a "human soul."

THE ORATOR

ONE fine morning, they were burying the Collegiate Assessor, Kyril Ivanovitch Vavilonov. He had died of two diseases both wide-spread in our motherland, alcoholism, and a nagging wife. While the funeral procession was setting out from the church to the cemetery, a colleague of the dead man, one Poplavski, got into a droshki and drove at a gallop to the house of his friend Grigori Petrovitch Zapoikin, a young man who was very popular. Zapoikin possessed a rare talent for delivering impromptu speeches at weddings, anniversaries and funerals. He could make a speech at any time, within seconds of waking, during burning fever, on an empty stomach, or while dead-drunk. His speech flowed evenly, smoothly, exactly like water flowing out of a pipe, and as abundantly. There were more sorrowful words in his oratorical vocabulary than blackbeetles in a dirty inn. He invariably spoke with eloquence, and at such length that sometimes, especially at shopkeepers' weddings, they had to send for the police to stop him.

"Ah! You're just the fellow I want, my lad," Poplavski began, on reaching the house. "Get dressed and come with me straight away. One of our chaps at the office has died; we're just packing him off to the next world, and somebody has to spout some kind of twaddle, you know, before we send him off. You're our only hope. If it was one of the small fry we wouldn't have bothered you, but it's the secretary, a pillar of the office, so to speak. You can't bury that kind of a nob without a speech."

"The secretary," yawned Zapoikin, "that the one who drinks?"

"Yes, he certainly did put it away. There'll be pancakes and plenty to eat. It won't cost you a kopek. Let's go, my dear man! When we get to the cemetery, you hold forth and out-Cicero Cicero, and you'll be the man of the hour!"

Zapoikin readily agreed. He ruffled his hair, put on a melancholy expression, and followed Poplavski into the street. "I know your secretary," he said, sitting in the droshki. "A rogue and a swindler, the Kingdom of Heaven be his! There are few like him."

"Hey, Grisha, you aren't supposed to run down the dead."

"Yes, I know. *De mortuis nihil nisi bonum.* But he was a scoundrel anyway."

The neighbours overtook and joined the funeral procession. The coffin was borne so slowly that they managed three times to slip into the tavern, and send down a small glass apiece for the repose of the departed soul.

At the grave-side the requiem had ended. The widow, mother-in-law, and sister-in-law, faithful to the custom, wept copiously. As the coffin was lowered into the grave the widow even cried out: "Let me go to him!" but, perhaps mindful of the pension, decided not to go. Zapoikin waited till calm had been restored, and then stepped forward, drawing all eyes, and began:

"Can we believe our eyes and ears? Are not this tomb, these weeping faces, these sobs and groans, a part of some terrible dream? Alas! It is no dream. Our eyes do not deceive us! He, whom only lately we saw in the pure, fresh, bloom of youth, who so lately before our eyes, like an indefatigable bee, bore his loads of honey to the common hive of Imperial well-being, is now turned to dust, to a material mirage. Inexorable death has laid its lingering hand on him, when, although crooked with age, he was still full of burgeoning power, and radiant hope. What an irreparable loss! Who will take his place among us? We have many capable officials, but Prokofi Ossipitch was unique. With his

whole soul he was devoted to the honest performance of
his duty; he never spared himself, he spent sleepless
nights, he was disinterested and incorruptible. How he
detested those who, in defiance of the common weal,
tried to bribe him; who, with tempting offers of the good
things of life, strove to involve him in betrayal of his
duty! Indeed, before our eyes Prokofi Ossipitch would
distribute his meagre salary to his poorer comrades, and
you yourselves have heard the sobs of widows and orphans
wiped away by charity. Entirely devoted to his official
duties and his good works, he knew none of the joys of
life, and even cut himself off from the felicity of family
life; as you know, he remained single to the end of his
mortal span. And who will take his place as the comrade of us all? As if he were standing before me now,
I can see his tragic, clean-shaven features, turned to us
with a good-natured smile; as if he were speaking to me,
I can hear his soft, sympathetic, friendly voice. Peace to
your ashes, Prokofi Ossipitch! Take your rest, honest,
noble toiler!"

Zapoikin continued, but the listeners began to whisper
among themselves. Everyone liked the speech; it had
extracted a few tears; but there was something funny
about it. To begin with, it was quite incomprehensible
why the speaker should refer to the dead man as Prokofi
Ossipitch, when his name was Kyril Ivanovitch. In the
second place, everybody knew that the dead man had
been at war with his lawful spouse all his life, and
certainly was not unmarried. Then again, he had a
thick red beard, and as he had never shaved in his life,
it was not clear why he was said to be clean-shaven.
The hearers exchanged wondering looks, and shrugged
their shoulders.

"Prokofi Ossipitch," the orator went on, looking
emotionally into the grave, "your features were plain,
even ugly, you were aloof and morose, but we all knew
that under your skin there beat a true and friendly heart."

All of a sudden the listeners began to notice how strangely the orator was behaving. He was staring fixedly at one point, and fidgeting nervously. Suddenly he broke off his speech, opened his mouth in surprise, and turned round to Poplavski.

" Look ! He's alive ! " he said, with terror in his eyes.

" Who's alive?"

" Prokofi Ossipitch. There he is by the monument."

" But he didn't die. It's Kyril Ivanovitch that's dead."

" But you told me your secretary was dead."

" Kyril Ivanovitch was our secretary. You got it all mixed up, you clown ! Prokofi Ossipitch certainly used to be our secretary, but he was transferred to the second section as chief clerk a couple of years ago."

" I can't make it out."

" What are you stopping for ? Go on, go on."

Zapoikin turned to the grave, and continued his interrupted oration with the same volubility. By the monument stood Prokofi Ossipitch, an old, clean-shaven official. He looked at the speaker with a wrathful scowl.

" What made you do that?" laughed the officials, when they were returning with Zapoikin from the funeral. " You buried a living man !"

" You did wrong, young man," growled Prokofi Ossipitch. " Your speech may have been suitable for a dead man, but for a living one it was sheer mockery, sir ! To say such things ! Disinterested ! Incorruptible ! Never take bribes ! That can only be said of a living person in mockery ! And nobody asked you to make remarks about my face ! Plain and ugly it may be, but why say so in public? It's insulting, sir ! "

ANTON CHEKHOV

THE SAFETY-MATCH

A STUDY IN CRIMINOLOGY

ON the morning of October 6th, 1885, there appeared in the office of the commissioner of rural police for the second circumscription of the district of S. a decently dressed young man who declared that his employer, the retired Guards officer Mark Ivanovich Klyauzov, had been murdered. The young man, as he made his declaration, was pale and extremely agitated. His hands trembled and his eyes were filled with horror.

"With whom have I the honour of speaking?" asked the commissioner.

"My name is Psekov, and I am . . . was Klyauzov's estate-agent. By profession I am an agriculturist and civil engineer."

The commissioner, reaching the scene of the occurrence accompanied by Psekov and the witnesses always recruited on such occasions, found that a crowd had gathered in the neighbourhood of the house in which Klyauzov lived. News of the crime had spread with the speed of lightning, and as it was a holiday peasants had streamed there from all the surrounding villages. Loud voices and a general commotion could be heard. Here and there pale, tear-stained faces were to be observed. The door leading to Klyauzov's ground-floor bedroom had been found locked. The key was inside.

"The murderers must have made their way in through the window," remarked Psekov as the door was being examined.

They went into the garden on which the bedroom window looked. The window had a gloomy and

ominous expression. It was hung with a faded green
curtain. One corner of the curtain was slightly displaced,
so that it was possible to see into the room.

"Have any of you looked in through the window?"
asked the commissioner.

"That we hain't, Your Honour," said Yefrem the
gardener, a little old man with gray hair and the face of
a retired N.C.O. "You don't go looking in at windows
when you're scared stiff!"

"Ah, Mark Ivanych, Mark Ivanych!" sighed the commissioner, looking at the window. "Didn't I keep telling
you that you'd come to a bad end? If I said it once I said
it a hundred times—but would he listen to me? Loose
living can only end in one way!"

"We have Yefrem to thank," said Psekov; "but for
him we shouldn't have realized that something was amiss.
He was the first to smell a rat. He came to me this
morning and said: 'How is it the master is so long in
getting up? Hasn't been out of his bedroom for a whole
week!' The moment he said this I felt as though I had
been hit on the head with a chopper . . . A thought
flashed into my mind . . . He hadn't shown up since
last Saturday, and now it was this Sunday! Seven days—
very fishy!"

"Poor fellow!" sighed the commissioner again. "A
clever chap, well-educated, good-natured . . . The life
and soul of the party, to coin a phrase. But such a libertine. God rest his soul! I always expected something like
this!—Stepan," he went on, addressing one of the witnesses, "dash back to my place and send Andrew to the
police-captain to tell him that Mark Ivanych has been
murdered. And run along to the police-sergeant too—
what the deuce does he think he's up to? He must come
here straight away. And then you can call at the examining magistrate's and tell Nikolay Yermolavich to come
along. Wait a minute—I'll write him a note."

The commissioner set guards round the wing in which

Klyanzov had lived, wrote a note to the examining magistrate and went to have a cup of tea with Psekov. Ten minutes later he was sitting on a stool, cautiously nibbling at a lump of sugar and gulping down the red-hot tea.

" You see," he said. " You see. A nobleman, wealthy . . . a favourite of the gods as you might say, quoting Pushkin; and what has come of him? Nothing at all! He drank, he went on the loose, and now . . . he's gone and got murdered!"

Two hours later the examining magistrate drove up. Nikolay Yermolayevich Chubikov (for this was the magistrate's name), a tall, stout old man of about sixty, had been pursuing his profession for a quarter of a century. He was known to the whole district as a man of honour, intelligent, industrious and keen on his job. He arrived at the scene of the crime accompanied by his assistant Dyukovsky, a tall young man of about twenty-six.

" God bless my soul!" exclaimed Chubikov, entering the room and hurriedly shaking hands with all present. " Who ever would have thought it? Mark Ivanych? Murdered? It's impossible! Im-poss-ible!"

" Only too possible, I'm afraid," sighed the commissioner.

" But heavens alive, I saw him just over a week ago at the Tarabankovo fair! As a matter of fact I had a drop of vodka with·him!"

" I don't doubt it," sighed the commissioner.

They all sighed, expressed their horror, drank a glass of tea and trooped to the scene of the crime.

" Make way!" cried the police-sergeant.

Entering the house, the examining magistrate commenced by studying the bedroom door. It proved to be of pine-wood, painted yellow and undamaged. There were no marks that might have served as clues. Thereupon they proceeded to break it open.

" I must beg those not directly concerned to go away,"

said the examining magistrate, when after a long banging
and cracking the door had yielded to axe and chisel. " In
the interests of justice . . . Sergeant, see that no one
comes in !"

Chubikov, his assistant and the commissioner pushed
open the door and one after the other, hesitatingly, entered
the bedroom. The following scene met their eyes. By
the window there was a large wooden bedstead with a
huge feather-bed. On the crumpled bed lay a crumped
quilt. A pillow in a cotton pillowcase, also very crumpled,
lay on the floor. On the small table by the bed were a
silver watch and a silver coin to the value of twenty
kopecks; also some sulphur matches. Apart from the bed,
the table and one chair there was no furniture in the room.
Looking under the bed, the commissioner perceived about
a score of empty bottles, an old straw hat and a small flask
of vodka. Beneath the table lay a dusty boot. Glancing
round the room, the examining magistrate frowned and
flushed.

" The scoundrels !" he muttered, clenching his fists.

" And where is Mark Ivanych ?" asked Dyukovsky in
a low voice.

" Please don't interrupt !" said Chubikov rudely. " See
what you can make of the floor ! This is the second case
of the sort in my experience, Yevgraf Kuzmich," he went
on to the commissioner. " Fifteen years ago I had to deal
with an identical business. I'm sure you'll remember . . .
The murder of the merchant Portretov. Exactly the same.
The rascals murdered him and dragged the corpse through
the window . . ."

Chubikov went over to the window, pulled the curtain
aside and gave the window a cautious poke. It opened.

" So it wasn't fastened . . . Hm ! . . . Traces on the
sill. You see ? The marks of knees . . . Someone crawled
through . . . We shall have to give the window a thorough
examination."

" Nothing special on the floor," said Dyukovsky. " No

stains, no scratches. All I have found is a burnt safety-match. Here it is! As far as I remember, Mark Ivanych did not smoke; and when he used matches they were sulphur ones and not safety. This may be a clue . . ."

"Do shut up!" cried the examining magistrate, waving his hand impatiently. "All this fuss about a match! I can't bear fussers! Instead of looking for matches you ought to have a good look at the bed!"

After examining the bed Dyukovsky reported:

"No bloodstains or any other stains . . . No recent tears in the material, either. On the pillow there are toothmarks. The quilt is soaked with a fluid smelling and tasting of beer . . The general appearance of the bed permits one to conclude that it was the scene of a struggle."

"I don't need to be told that there was a struggle! Nobody's asking you about struggles. Instead of looking for struggles, you'd be better occupied—"

"One boot is here; the other is missing."

"What of it?"

"It means that he was suffocated while he was taking his boots off. He had only taken one off when—"

"Stuff and nonsense! And how do you know that he was suffocated?"

"From the toothmarks on the pillow. The pillow itself is very crumpled, and is lying five feet ten inches from the bed."

"The way the fellow chatters! We'd do better to go into the garden. Have a good look round the garden, you, instead of messing about in here . . . I can do that quite well myself."

Entering the garden they first proceeded to examine the grass beneath the window. It was crushed. A burdock growing just by the wall was also crushed. Dyukovsky succeeded in discovering among the leaves a few snapped twigs and a piece of cotton wool; also some threads of dark blue material.

L

" What colour was his suit?" Dyukovsky asked Psekov.

" Brown."

" Splendid! The murderers were wearing blue."

Several heads of burdock were cut off and carefully wrapped in paper. At this moment they were joined by Artsybashev-Svistovsky the police-captain and Doctor Tyutyuyev. The police-captain said How-do and proceeded to satisfy his curiosity, while the doctor, a tall and extremely thin man with sunken eyes, a long nose and a sharp chin, greeting no one, asking no questions, sat down on a tree-stump, sighed and said:

" Those Serbs causing difficulties again! Can't conceive what they're after! Ah, Austria, Austria! Your fingers are in this!"

An examination of the window from outside produced no results; but scrutiny of the grass and the bushes nearest to the house provided many clues. For instance, Dyukovsky discovered in the grass a dark trail of spots leading from the window some way into the garden. It ended in a large dark-brown spot beneath one of the lilac-bushes. By the same bush they found a boot matching the one found in the bedroom.

" This is blood that has been here some time," said Dyukovsky, examining the spots.

At the word " blood " the doctor stood up and glanced lazily at the stains.

" Blood," he mumbled. " You're quite right."

" That means he wasn't suffocated," said Chubikov, looking poisonously at Dyukovsky.

" They suffocated him in the bedroom and then, fearing he might recover, struck him out here with a sharp object. The stains beneath the lilac-bush show that he lay there for a relatively long time; meanwhile the murderers were looking for a way out of the garden and something to carry the corpse on."

" And what about the boot?"

" This boot further corroborates my theory that he was killed while he was taking his boots off. One boot was quite off, while the other one, that is to say this one, was still half on. While he was being dragged along, the partly unlaced boot became dislodged . . ."

" How he thinks it all out!" sneered Chubikov. " On and on! When *will* you learn not to be so forward with your theories? Rather than theorize, you would be better engaged collecting some of the blood-stained grass for subsequent analysis!"

After concluding their examination and making a plan of the premises they proceeded to Psekov's place to write a report and have lunch. Over lunch they talked.

" Watch, money *et cetera* all accounted for," began Chubikov. " It's as clear as day that the murder was not committed for gain."

" And that the criminal was of the upper classes," put in Dyukovsky.

" What makes you think that?"

" The safety-match, an object not used by the local peasants. Such matches are only used by the landowners, and not by all of them for that matter. Incidentally, the murder was committed by not one but at least three persons : two held the victim while the third suffocated him. Klyauzov was a strong man, and the murderers must have been aware of this."

"What use would his strength have been if, let us suppose, he was asleep? "

" But they came upon him when he was taking his boots off. If he was taking his boots off he wasn't asleep."

" What an imagination! You'd be better occupied eating your lunch!"

" And in my opinion, Your Honour," said Yefrem the gardener, who was placing the samovar on the table, " the one who done it was none other than Nikolashka."

" Quite possible," said Psekov.

"And who may Nikolashka be?"

"The master's man, Your Honour," replied Yefrem. "Who is more likely to have done it? A regular bandit, Your Honour. Such a drunkard and womanizer you never did see! He used to take the master vodka, he used to put him to bed . . . Who else can have done it? What's more, if I may be permitted to inform Your Honour, he once boasted, the rogue, that he'd do for the master. It was all because of Hannah, all because of that woman . . . A soldier's wife, she is . . Took the master's fancy, so he took her . . . And—stands to reasons—Nikolashka took it badly . . . Now he's lying drunk in the kitchen, snivelling . . . Says he's sorry for the master . . ."

"It's a fact that he had reason to feel sore about Hannah," said Psekov. "Just a soldier's wife, but . . . Not for nothing did Mark Ivanych call her Nana after Zola's heroine. There certainly is something about her that reminds you of Nana . . something alluring . . ."

"I've seen her . . . I know . . ." said the examining magistrate, blowing his nose in a red handkerchief.

Dyukovsky blushed and lowered his gaze. The commissioner drummed on the table. The police-captain burst out coughing and started groping for something in his brief-case. The doctor seemed to be the only one on whom the reference to Hannah and Nana had made no impression. The examining magistrate ordered Nikolashka to be brought in, and Nikolashka, a young gangling lad with a long pock-marked nose and a sunken chest, wearing a jacket from his master's back, entered Psekov's room and bowed low before the examining magistrate. His face was sleepy and tear-stained. He was drunk, and could hardly stand.

"Where is your master?" asked Chubikov sternly.

"They've done him in, Your Honour."

Saying this, Nikolashka blinked his eyes and started weeping.

" We know. But where is he now? Where is the corpse?"

" They say he was dragged through the window and buried in the garden."

" Hm! . . . I see that the kitchen already knows all about the results of our enquiries . . . Bad, bad! Tell me, my man, where were you on the night your master was killed? On the Saturday? "

Nikolashka raised his face towards the ceiling, stretched his neck and thought profoundly.

" I couldn't say, Your Honour," he brought out at length. " I'd had a drop; I can't remember."

" An alibi!" whispered Dyukovsky, smiling and rubbing his hands.

" I see. And how is it that there are bloodstains under your master's window?"

Nikolashka threw his head back and pondered.

" Come on, think!" said the police-captain.

" Yessir. Well now, that there blood don't mean a thing, Your Honour. I'd been killing a hen. I was just cutting her head off, same as usual, then she flew out of my hands and started flerricking all over the place . . . It's her blood, that there hen's."

Yefrem confirmed that Nikolashka was in the habit of killing poultry every evening and in various places, but no one had observed an imperfectly decapitated hen running about the garden; however, this possibility could not be quite ruled out.

" An alibi," laughed Dyukovsky. " And what a stupid one!"

" Did you have anything to do with the woman Hannah?"

" Guilty, Your Honour."

" And your master seduced her from you?"

" Not at all. Hannah was took away from me by *him*, by Mr. Psekov there, and the master took her away from *him*. That's how it was."

Psekov was embarrassed, and started rubbing his left eye. Dyukovsky looked keenly at him, read the confusion in his face and gave a start. He observed something he had not noticed before: the young man was wearing blue trousers. He thought of the blue strands found in the burdock. Chubikov too glanced suspiciously at Psekov.

"Leave the room!" he said to Nikolashka. "And now, Mr. Psekov, allow me to put you a question. On the night of Saturday to Sunday you, of course, were here?"

"Yes. At ten o'clock I had supper with Mark Ivanych."

"And then?"

Psekov, perturbed, rose from the table.

"Then . . . then . . . I really can't remember," he mumbled. "I'd had a lot of drink . . . I can't remember where and when I went to sleep . . . Why are you looking at me like that? Anyone would think *I'd* murdered him!"

"Where did you wake up?"

"On the stove in the kitchen .. . . All the servants will confirm this. How I came to be on the stove I just don't know . . ."

"Don't get agitated! . . . You knew Hannah?"

"There wasn't anything in that . . ."

"And she left you for Klyauzov?"

"That is so. Yefrem, give me some more mushrooms! Will you have some tea, Yevgraf Kuzmich?"

Silence fell, a heavy, creepy silence that lasted about five minutes. Dyukovsky said nothing, his eyes fastened on Psekov's pale face. The examining magistrate was first to speak.

"We must go over to the main building and have a word with Marya Ivanovna, the sister of the deceased. Perhaps she will be able to throw some light on the matter."

Chubikov and his assistant said thank-you for their lunch and went over to the main building. There they found Marya Ivanovna Klyauzova, a spinster of forty-five, on her knees before the tall ancestral ikon-case. Seeing that her visitors had brief-cases in their hands and uniform caps on their heads, she turned pale.

"I must first apologise, madam, for disturbing you, so to speak, at your prayers," began the gallant Chubikov, clicking his heels. "We have a request to make you. You have of course already heard . . . There is a suspicion that your poor brother was, in a manner of speaking, murdered . . . We are all in the hands of God . . . No one can escape his death, neither emperor nor ploughman. But perhaps you will be able to help us clear up the mystery. Please think carefully."

"Oh, don't ask me!" said Marya Ivanovna, turning still paler and covering her face with her hands. "There's nothing I can tell you! Nothing! Please don't ask! What can I tell you? I won't say anything about my brother—not a word! I'd sooner die than tell!"

Marya Ivanovna burst into tears and rushed from the room. The men exchanged glances, shrugged their shoulders and withdrew.

"A devil of a woman!" swore Dyukovsky as they left the house. "It's as plain as the nose on your face that she knows something and won't talk. And there was something suspicious about the parlour-maid's expression, too . . . Just wait, you devils! We'll get to the bottom of this!"

That evening Chubikov and his assistant were returning home in the pale light of the moon; they sat in their gig summing up in their heads the events of the day. Both were tired and wordless. Chubikov was always rather taciturn when travelling, and the talkative Dyukovsky was silent out of respect for his superior. But when they were nearing home he could remain silent no longer:

"That the fellow Nikolashka is implicated in this affair," he said, "*non dubitandum est*. You can tell by his ugly mug the sort of chap he is . . . His alibi hands him over tied up in a parcel. But there's also no question that he was not the instigator of the crime. He was merely a stupid, suborned tool. Do you agree? Nor is the least significant of rôles in this affair played by the modest Psekov. His blue trousers, his embarrassment, his lying on the stove filled with fear after the murder, his alibi, Hannah . . ."

"Young man, you're simply wonderful! So, according to you, whoever knew Hannah is the murderer? My poor fellow! You ought to be sucking a dummy, not investigating crimes! I seem to remember that you too had your eye on Hannah; so you too are involved?"

"For that matter Hannah worked in your kitchen for a month, but . . . I'm not suggesting anything. That Saturday evening I was playing cards with you; I know where you were; otherwise you would be on the list of suspects. The point, my dear sir, is not the woman Hannah. The point is a vile, beastly, loathsome feeling . . . The modest young man, you see, didn't like being pushed out into the cold. Vanity, you know . . . He wanted his revenge. And then . . . His thick lips speak sensuality. You remember how he smacked them when he was comparing Hannah with Nana? That he is a scoundrel, devoured by passion, is unquestionable! And so: injured vanity and unsatisfied passion. Quite sufficient to make one a murderer. Two of the culprits are in our hands; but who is the third? Nikolashka and Psekov held him while he was being suffocated. But who did the suffocating? Psekov is timid, easily confused, a coward generally. People like Nikolashka don't go in for suffocating with pillows; they use things like axes . . . The killer was a third party; but who?"

Dyukovsky pulled his hat down over his eyes and pondered. He said nothing more till the gig drew up before the examining magistrate's house.

"*Eureka!*" he cried when he had entered the little house and was pulling off his overcoat. "I've got it, Nikolay Yermolayich! I can't think how it didn't occur to me before! Do you know who the third one is?"

"Leave me in peace for goodness' sake! See, supper is ready. Eat what's given you and stop bothering me!"

The examining magistrate and Dyukovsky sat down and had supper. Dyukovsky poured himself a glass of vodka, stood up, stretched, and said, his eyes sparkling:

"The third party, you see, the one who joined forces with the rascally Psekov and did the suffocating—was a woman! You hear? I mean the sister of the deceased, Marya Ivanovna!"

Chubikov swallowed some vodka the wrong way, coughed, and glared at Dyukovsky.

"You're feeling all right, I suppose? Your head . . . not aching, by any chance? How's your pulse?"

"Don't worry, I'm quite right in the head. But even if I were crazy, how do you explain her confusion when we arrived? Her refusal to say anything? And if these things mean nothing, well and good: just cast your mind back to their relations with one another. She hated her brother, you know! She is a pious spinster, he a libertine, an unbeliever . . . Plenty of reasons for her to hate him! It's said that he had succeeded in persuading her that he was a sort of terrestrial deputy for Satan. And he used to go in for table-turning in her presence."

"What of it?"

"Don't you understand? She killed him out of religious mania! Not only was she rooting out the tares, destroying a libertine; she was delivering the world from Antichrist. This was, in her crazy mind, her great merit, her deed of religious derring-do. You've no idea what goes on in the minds of those old maids, those religious cranks! Remember the way Dostoevsky writes about them; and Leskov, and Pechersky! . . . She's the one, take

my word for it! She was the killer! The *femme fatale!*
Wasn't that why she was praying before the ikons when
we came in—just to pull the wool over our eyes? I'll
pretend to be praying, she must have thought, and those
poor fools will think that I'm quite calm, that I wasn't
expecting them to come bursting in! That's the way all
beginners in crime behave. Nikolay Yermolayich, let me
take charge of the case! Please! I began it; let me see it
through to the end!"

Chubikov shook his head and frowned.

"We ourselves know how to deal with difficult cases,"
he said. "And your business is not to poke your nose into
what isn't your business. Take down from dictation when
you're dictated to—that's your job!"

Dyukovsky flared up and went out, slamming the door.

"He's a clever lad, the rogue!" muttered Chubikov,
watching Dyukovsky disappear. "Knows a thing or two.
A pity he's so hot-headed! Next time I'm at a fair I must
get him a cigar-case for a present . . ."

Next morning there arrived from Klyauzovka, for
examination by the magistrate, a lad with a large head
and a hare-lip who, having announced himself as Daniel
the shepherd, told a very interesting story.

"I'd been drinking," he said. "Sat up with my god-
mother till midnight. On the way home, drunk like, went
down to the river to have a dip. While I was splashing
about, what do I see coming along the bank but two men
carrying something black. 'Hey!' I calls out to them.
They got the wind up and dashed off towards the market-
gardens. So help me God if it weren't the master they
was dragging along."

That evening Psekov and Nikolashka were arrested
and sent under convoy to the district town. There they
were put under lock and key.

II

Twelve days passed.

It was morning. The examining magistrate was sitting

at his green-covered table turning over the pages of the
Klyauzov dossier. Dyukovsky was pacing restlessly up
and down like a caged beast.

"You are convinced of the guilt of Nikolashka and
Psekov," said Dyukovsky, nervously fingering his young
beard. "Why aren't you equally prepared to accept the
guilt of Marya Ivanovna? Insufficient evidence?"

"I don't say I'm not convinced. I *am* convinced, but
somehow I can't believe it . . . There is no real evidence;
just a sort of theory-spinning. Religious mania and Lord
knows what . . ."

"And you of course must be able to lay your hands on
hatchets and bloodstained sheets! . . . Lawyers! Well,
I'll prove that I'm right! I'll make you stop taking such
a lackadaisical view of the psychological side of the case!
Your Marya Ivanovna shall go to Siberia! I'll prove her
guilt! If psychology is not enough for you, I have something material to go on . . . Something that will prove
to you how right my philosophy is! Just let me take the
gig round a bit."

"What material evidence are you talking about?"

"The safety-match . . . Had you forgotten it?
I hadn't! I will find out who struck it in the dead man's
room! It wasn't lit by Nikolashka or by Psekov, on
neither of whom matches were found, but by a third
party; and that third party was Marya Ivanovna. Just
you wait; I'll prove it! . . . Just you let me drive round
the district a bit . . ."

"All right, all right; do sit down for goodness' sake!
We must make out our report."

Dyukovsky sat down and plunged his long nose in
his papers.

"Bring in Nikolay Tetekhov!" called the examining
magistrate.

Nikolashka was led in. He was pale, and thin as a lath.
He was all of a tremble.

"Tetekhov!" began Chubikov. "Six years ago you

were convicted of theft in the court of the first circumscription and condemned to a term of imprisonment.
Three years later you were tried for theft for a second
time, and for a second time sent to jail. You see, we
know everything."

Nikolashka's face expressed surprise. The omniscience
of the examining magistrate amazed him. But soon his
surprise was replaced by an expression of profound
sorrow. He burst into sobs and begged permission to go
and wash his face and calm down. His request was
granted.

"Bring in Psekov!" ordered the examining magistrate.

Psekov was led in. In the last few days the young man's
face had changed considerably. It was thin, pale and
sunken. His eyes held an apathetic expression.

"Sit down, Psekov," said Chubikov. "I trust that
this time you will be sensible and cut out the lies. All the
other times you denied your complicity in the murder
of Klyauzov, despite the evidence against you. That
wasn't wise. Confession mitigates the crime. Today
I am speaking to you for the last time. If you don't
confess today, tomorrow will be too late. Come, tell us
the whole story!"

"I don't know a thing . . . I don't know anything
about the evidence you say you have," whispered Psekov.

"It's no good, I tell you! Permit me to narrate the
course of events. On the Saturday evening you were
sitting in Klyauzov's bedroom drinking vodka and beer."
(Dyukovsky plunged his gaze into Psekov's face and kept
it there during the whole time Chubikov was talking).
"Nikolay was serving you. At some time between
twelve and one, Mark Ivanovich expressed the desire to
go to bed. He always went to bed between twelve and
one. When he was taking off his boots and giving you
instructions, you and Nikolay at a prearranged sign
seized your intoxicated master and threw him on to the
bed. One of you sat on his legs, the other on his head.

At that moment there came in from the passage a woman you know, a woman in black who had previously arranged with you regarding the part she was to play in the baneful deed. She seized a pillow and began to suffocate him with it. In the course of the struggle the candle went out. The woman took a box of safety-matches from her pocket and relit the candle. Wasn't it so? I can see by your face that my narrative corresponds to the facts. However . . . Having suffocated him and convinced yourselves that he was no longer breathing, you and Nikolay dragged him through the window and laid him down by the burdock. Fearing lest he might revive, you struck him with a sharp object. Then you carried him over to the lilac-bush and left him there for a while. When you had rested and made your plans, you took him up again . . . Carried him along the road . . . Then came the river-bank. There you were startled by a peasant.—What's the matter?"

Psekov, pale as a sheet, rose from his chair and staggered a few paces.

"I'm suffocating!" he cried. "All right . . . Have it your own way . . . But I must go outside for a while . . . Please let me!"

Psekov was led out.

"So he's owned up at last!" said Chubikov, stretching luxuriousy. "Gave himself away! Still, I think I handled him rather cleverly. Showed him that I knew everything . . ."

"And he doesn't deny the existence of the woman in black!" laughed Dyukovsky. "But I'm terribly puzzled by the safety-match. I can't bear it any longer. Good-bye. I'm off."

Dyukovsky put on his uniform cap and drove off. Chubikov began to interrogate the woman Hannah. Hannah declared firmly that she didn't know nothing about nothing.

"I only lived with you, and with no one else," she

asserted.

Between five and six Dyukovsky returned. He was agitated as never before. His hands were trembling so that he was unable to unbutton his greatcoat. His cheeks were burning. One could see that he had not returned empty-handed.

"*Veni, vidi, vici!*" he said, flying into Chubikov's room and falling into an armchair. "I swear I'm beginning to believe in my own genius! Listen to me, devil take you! Listen and be amazed, old man! It's both funny and sad! We already hold three suspects, don't we? Well, I've found a fourth, and like the third she's a woman! And what a woman! To touch her shoulders once I would give ten years of my life! . . . But listen! I drove out to Klyauzovka and began to describe a spiral round it Following my spiral I visited all the shops, inns, wine-cellars in the district, asking everywhere for safety-matches. Everywhere I was told that they hadn't any in stock. I kept on keeping on. Twenty times I gave up hope and as often recovered it again. All day I wandered about, and not till an hour ago did I hit on what I was looking for. Three versts away from here. They gave me a packet of ten boxes. One of the boxes was missing. Who bought that box? Such and such a lady; she liked them because they go *psh!*—Old man! Nikolay Yermolayich! It's incredible what a man can do who was expelled from a seminary and knows the works of Gaboriau by heart! From now on I shall respect myself! . . . By Jove! Well, let's get going!"

"Where?"

"To call on her, the fourth suspect . . . We must hurry, otherwise . . . otherwise I shall boil over with impatience! Do you know who she is? You'll never guess! The young wife of the worthy Yevgraf Kuzmich, our police commissioner! Olga Petrovna—none other! She was the purchaser of the matches!"

"You . . . you . . . Have you gone out of your senses?"

"Not at all! It's quite simple. In the first place, she smokes cigarettes. Secondly, she was head over heels in love with Klyauzov. He rejected her advances, preferring the embraces of a certain Hannah of whom you may have heard. A woman scorned . . . Now I remember finding them once behind the screen in the kitchen. She was on her knees before him, and he was smoking her cigarette and puffing the smoke in her face. But what are we talking for? Let's be off before it gets dark. Come on!"

"I'm not yet sufficiently crazy to go bothering a respectable lady in the middle of the night because of the idle chatter of a milksop like you!"

"Respectable? After this you're not an examining magistrate, but nothing more nor less than an old washing-bag! Never before have I dared to speak my mind about you, but now you make me! You old bag! You moth-eaten dressing-gown! Please, Nikolay Yermolayich! I beg you!"

The examining magistrate waved his hand despairingly and spat in disgust.

"Please! I'm asking not for myself, but in the interests of justice. D'you want me to go down on my knees? Just for once, do what I ask you!"

And Dyukovsky sank to his knees.

"Nikolay Yermolayich! Have a heart! You can call me what you like if I'm mistaken regarding that woman. Remember that this is a case of murder! And what a case! It's like something out of a book! We shall be famous all over Russia! They'll make you chief examining magistrate. Please be sensible, you stupid old man!"

The examining magistrate frowned and put out a hesitant hand for his hat.

"Damn your eyes!" he said gloomily. "Let's get going, then!"

It was already dark when the magistrate's gig drew up before the commissioner's residence.

"What swine we are!" said Chubikov as he took hold of the bell-pull. "Disturbing people like this!"

"It's all right! Don't lose your nerve! We'll say that one of the gig-springs has gone."

Chubikov and Dyukovsky were admitted by a tall, plump woman of about twenty-three with pitch-black eyebrows and puffed red lips. It was Olga Petrovna in person.

"What a pleasant surprise!" she said, smiling all over her face. "Just in time for supper. My husband is not at home. He's over at the priest's . . . Never mind, we can get on quite nicely without him . . . Please come in and sit down. Have you been out investigating and so forth?"

"Yes. And one of our sprig-gings . . . our gig-springs has been naughty enough to go phut," began Chubikov, entering the drawing-room and settling down in an armchair.

"Shoot it out at her!" whispered Dyukovsky. "Stun her!"

"A grig-sping, as I say . . . We were rolling along, and suddenly . . ."

"Let her have it, I tell you! If you talk nonsense like that she'll guess that something is up!"

"Well, do as you think best, and let me out of this!" said Chubikov, rising from his chair and approaching the window. "I just can't bring myself to . . . You cooked the kasha, so you can eat it!"

"A spring-gig went, as Nikolay Yermolayich was saying . . ." began Dyukovsky, going over to the commissioner's wife and wrinkling his long nose. "We weren't coming here for . . . ahem . . . supper, or to see Yevgraf Kuzmich. Our object in coming was to ask you, madam, where Mark Ivanovich is. You know, the man you did away with."

M

" What? What Mark Ivanovich? " stammered Olga Petrovna, and in a moment her broad face was flooded with crimson. " I . . . I don't understand . . . "

" In the name of the law! Where is Klyauzov? We know everything! "

" Who told you? " asked Olga Petrovna, unable to bear Dyukovsky's piercing gaze.

" Please show us where he is."

" But how did you know? Who told you? "

" We know e-ve-ry-thing! In the name of the law! "

The examining magistrate, encouraged by the lady's obvious confusion, went up to her and said :

" Show us, and we'll go away. Otherwise we . . . "

" What do you want him for? "

" Why these questions, madam? We want to be shown the victim. You are trembling, perturbed . . . Yes, he has been done away with; and if you must know, by you! Your accomplices have betrayed you! "

The commissioner's wife turned pale.

" Come," she said quietly, wringing her hands. " He's hidden in the old bath-house. But for God's sake don't tell my husband! I beseech you! He would never get over it."

She took a large key from the wall and led her visitors through the kitchen into the courtyard. It was dark. There was a drizzle of rain. The woman went on ahead. Chubikov and Dyukovsky tramped in her wake through the tall grass, inhaling the aroma of wild hemp and the kitchen-slops sighing beneath their feet. Soon the slops came to an end, and the feet felt ploughed soil beneath them. Out of the darkness loomed the silhouettes of trees, and between the trees appeared a little building with a crooked chimney.

" This is the old bath-house," said the commissioner's wife. " But I beseech you not to tell anyone!'"

Approaching the bath-house, Chubikov and Dyukovsky beheld on the door an enormous padlock.

"Get out a candle-end and some matches," whispered the examining magistrate to his assistant.

The commissioner's wife unlocked the door and let her visitors into the bath-house. Dyukovsky struck a match and lit up the outer chamber. In the middle stood a table. On the table, next to a tubby samovar, stood a tureen contained congealed cabbage-soup and a dish smeared with the traces of some sort of dressing.

"Come on!"

They went into the next chamber, the bathroom proper. Another table. On the table a large dish with a ham, a bottle of vodka, plates, knives and forks.

"But where is . . . um? Where is the victim?" asked the examining magistrate.

"On the upper steaming-shelf!" whispered the commissioner's wife, still pale and trembling.

Dyukovsky took the candle-end and climbed up to the steaming-shelf. There he perceived a long human form lying with the stillness of death on a large feather mattress. The form emitted a slight snoring sound. . .

"We've been had!" cried Dyukovsky. "This isn't a stiff! Some animated noodle is lying here. Hey, who are you, devil take you?"

The form drew in the air with a whistle and began to stir. Dyukovsky poked it with his elbow. It lifted its arms, stretched out its legs and raised its head.

"Who's that crawling about?" asked a hoarse bass. "What do you want?"

Dyukovsky brought the candle-end near to the face of the unknown, and gave a cry. In the crimson nose, the dishevelled locks, the pitch-black moustaches, one of which was dashingly twirled and pointed arrogantly at the ceiling, he recognised Mark Ivanovich Klyauzov, late of the Guards.

"Are . . . you . . . Mark Ivanych? You can't be!"

The examining magistrate shot a glance upwards and froze into stillness.

" Of course I am ! Is that you, Dyukovsky? What the devil do you want here? Whose is the mug down there? God bless my soul, it's the examining magistrate! What on earth has brought *you* here?"

Klyauzov crawled down and embraced Chubikov. Olga Petrovna made herself scarce.

"Well I'll be blowed! We must have a drink, damn it all! Ta-ra-ra-boom-de-ay . . . Come on, pour out! But who on earth brought you here? How did you find out I was up there? Still, what does it matter? We'll have a drink!"

Klyauzov lit a lamp and poured three glasses of vodka.

" I am quite at a loss," said the examining magistrate, spreading his arms helplessly. " Is it really you?"

" That'll do asking silly questions! Not going to read me a lecture, I hope! My young friend Dyukovsky, drink up! A short life and . . . What are you staring at! Come on, bottoms up!"

" But I really can't understand," said the examining magistrate, mechanically drinking his vodka, " what you are doing here."

" Why shouldn't I be here, if it suits me?"

Klyauzov emptied his glass and carved himself a slice of ham.

" As you see, I am living with the commissioner's wife. Hidden away, like a sort of domestic sprite. Drink up! I felt sorry for her, old man! Took pity on her, and now I'm living here, in an abandoned bath-house, like a sort of hermit . . . And on rather short commons. Next week I think I shall have to make tracks. Had enough of it."

" This is absolutely beyond everything!" said Dyukovsky.

" What's beyond what?"

" Everything! In heaven's name, how did your boot come to be in the garden?"

" What boot?"

"We found one boot in the bedroom and the other in the garden."

"Why should you know? No business of yours! Come on, swallow it down, devil take you! You disturbed me when I was having a nice nap, so now you must take the consequences! An interesting business, old man, that business of the boot. To tell you the truth I didn't want to come over to Olga's. A bit out of sorts, you know; under the weather . . . Well, Olga comes up to my window and starts arguing. You know how women are . . . the way they go on . . . Having had a drop, I let fly at her with a boot . . . Ha-ha! . . . Cut it out, so to say. She climbed in through the window, lit the lamp and started mawling me. Knocked me about, dragged me here and locked me up. And now I'm living on love, vodka and sliced ham.—But where are you off to? Chubikov, where are you going?"

The examining magistrate spat and left the bath-house. After him went Dyukovsky, his head hanging. Silently they sat in the gig and drove off. Never before had the road seemed so dull and never-ending. Neither said a word. All the way home Chubikov was trembling with fury; Dyukovsky hid his nose in his coat-collar as though afraid lest the darkness and the drizzling rain might read the shame in his face.

Reaching his house, the examining magistrate found Dr. Tyutyuyev waiting for him. The doctor was sitting at a table turning over the pages of a periodical and sighing deeply.

"The things that are going on!" he said, greeting the examining magistrate with a mournful smile. "Austria what's-its-naming again. And Gladstone too, in a manner of speaking . . ."

Chubikov threw his hat beneath the table and shook all over.

"You devilish skeleton! Keep out of my way! I've told you a thousand times not to come bothering me with your politics! I don't feel in the mood for politics!—And you," he turned to Dyukovsky and shook his fist at him, "you I shall never forget if I live to be a hundred!"

"But . . . it was a safety-match after all! How could I know. . . ."

"Go and swallow your safety-match! Go away and stop irritating me, or there's no knowing what I may do to you! I never want to set eyes on you again!"

Dyukovsky sighed, took his hat and went out. "I'll go and get drunk!" he resolved as he passed through the gate, and sadly he plodded pubwards.

When the commissioner's wife got back to the house she found her husband sitting in the drawing-room.

"Why did the examining magistrate call?" he asked.

"He came to say that Klyauzov has been found. Just think, he was with somebody else's wife!"

"Ah, Mark Ivanych!" sighed the commissioner, raising his eyes to the ceiling. "I told you that your loose living would bring you no good! I told you—but would you listen to me?"

MIKHAIL ZOSHCHENKO

IN HOSPITAL

TO be perfectly frank, I prefer to stay at home when I'm ill. Of course, there's no denying that in a hospital you are likely to get more light and more culture, and the calories and what not of the food you eat are all added up most carefully; but there's a lot to be said for being ill at home.

However, I did get taken to hospital once when I had

typhoid, and my people at home thought that by sending me to a hospital they could alleviate my sufferings so heroically borne. But it didn't work out that way at all at the particular hospital where I went: I can't really say I liked everything there.

Now I ask you, is it right for a patient who has just arrived and is having his name and so forth written down in a book to have to read a huge placard hanging on the wall: "Relatives should call for corpses between 3 and 4 p.m."? I don't know about other patients, but I felt myself swaying on my feet as I read this appeal. Here was I with life nearly extinct or perhaps just hanging by a hair, and to have such words dangling before my eyes!

I told the man who was writing down my particulars in a book:

"Comrade Doctor's Assistant, why do you have such vulgar inscriptions hanging on your walls?"

The doctor's assistant, or whoever he was, was surprised, and said:

"This is a pretty state of affairs! Here's a sick man who can hardly walk and practically with steam coming out of his mouth owing to a high temperature and yet well enough to go in for critical introspection. If you ever get well, which I very much doubt, then you can criticise to your heart's content; otherwise we'll hand you out to your relatives between three and four p.m. just as it says on the notice, and we'll see how you like that!"

I wanted to give the doctor's assistant a piece of my mind, but as my temperature was about 103 I didn't argue with him. I merely said:

"You just wait, you old stethoscope; let me get well and you'll answer for your impudence. Is that the way to talk to the sick?" I said. "Such conversations sap their moral strength."

The doctor's assistant was surprised that a man who

was so seriously ill should talk to him so freely, so he tried to change the topic. Just then a little nurse trotted up.

"Come on," she said to me, "follow me to have a wash-down."

Her words upset me more than I can say.

"It would be greatly preferable," I said, "if you alluded to a bath and not to a wash-down. It sounds better and is more in keeping with the patient's moral dignity. I am not a horse that has to be washed down!"

"I thought you were a sick man, and here you are making all sorts of genteel observations," said the nurse. "I don't suppose you will ever recover; that's why you want to stick your nose into everything."

She led me to the bathroom and told me to undress. I was beginning to get my things off when suddenly I saw there was a head sticking out of the bath-water. It looked to me very like an old woman—one of the patients, probably—having a bath.

"Look here," I said, "where have you nitwits brought me? Isn't this the ladies' bathroom? There seems to be someone having a bath here."

The nurse said:

"Well, there's a sick woman here if that's what you mean, but you needn't pay any attention to her. She has a high temperature and doesn't react to anything. So just get on with your undressing. By the time you are ready we'll have the old lady out and run a fresh bath for you."

I said:

"Maybe the old woman doesn't react, but what about me? I still happen to be in a condition to react; and," I said, "it's definitely unpleasant for me to look at what you have floating in that bath."

Suddenly the doctor's assistant came in.

"For the first time in all my born days," he said, "have I come across such a particular patient. He doesn't like this and he doesn't like that. He even objects to a dying woman having a bath. Maybe her temperature is about 104 and she is semi-conscious or can only see things quite hazily. And anyway let me tell you that if she does take a look at you what she'll see won't detain her in this world for as much as an extra five minutes. Give me patients every time," he said, " who are brought here unconscious. Then at all events everything is to their liking, they are satisfied with everything and don't enter into scientific controversies with us."

Here the old lady in the bath joined in the conversation.

" Get me out of here," she says, "or I shall come out myself and murder you all."

So they turned their attention to the old thing and told me to hurry up and get undressed. By the time I was ready they had filled the bath with hot water and I was told to get in.

By now they had realised what sort of man they had to deal with, so they did not argue with me any more, but rather tried to agree with all I said. Only when I had finished they gave me some enormous clothes that were far too big for me; at first I thought this was just out of spite, but later on I noticed this was just the way they did things at the hospital. All the little men wore things miles too big for them, and all the big patients were in clothes that were very tight.

As a matter of fact my outfit was better than what many of the others had; the hospital mark was on my sleeve and did not spoil the general effect, while others had the name stamped on their back, or on their chest, which is morally lowering to human dignity.

However, as my temperature continued to go up, I did not go in for any more arguments.

I was put in a small ward with some thirty patients of all kinds: some of them I should say were pretty ill; others on the other hand were definitely getting better;

some of them were whistling; some were playing
draughts; others wandered about the ward and tried to
spell out what was written on the cards above the
patients' heads.

I said to the nurse:

"Maybe I am in a lunatic asylum—you might as well
tell me so straight out. Every year of my life I have been
in a hospital, but never have I struck anything like this.
In other places one gets peace and quiet, but here you
might as well be in the middle of the market-place."

The nurse said:

"Perhaps you would like to be put in a private room
and have a sentry posted by your bed to drive away flies
and fleas."

I kicked up a row and said I wanted to see the doctor
in charge, but who should turn up but the same doctor's
assistant! I had been feeling pretty weak, but on seeing
him I just passed out. It must have been three days later
that I came to again. The nurse said to me:

"You must have an iron constitution and have come
through with flying colours. Once we even left you ac-
cidentally lying under an open window, and after that
you suddenly began to get better. Now, unless you catch
some infectious disease from patients in neighbouring
beds, we shall be able to congratulate you on a marvellous
recovery."

Well, my constitution did not succumb to any more
diseases after that, except that just as I was waiting for my
discharge I did catch a childish ailment—whooping
cough.

The nurse said: "You must have caught this from the
other block. That's where the children's wards are. All
I can think of is that you have carelessly eaten off a plate
used by a child suffering from whooping cough. That's
why you are not feeling well now."

Well, soon after this my constitution triumphed once
more, and I began to get better. But when it came to

getting myself discharged from the hospital I was once more faced with great suffering and fell ill again—this time with a nervous complaint: my body was covered with small pimples—a sort of nervous rash. The doctor said to me:

"Stop worrying, and with time the rash will disappear."

But what I was worrying about was not being able to get out of the hospital. Either they would forget all about me, or there was something missing that they should have, or someone should have come and done something, but hadn't come and couldn't do it. Till at last they had a large batch of new patients, and all the staff were rushed off their feet. The doctor's assistant said:

"We are too full up now to have any time to discharge those who have recovered. Also you must realise that you have been well only for the last eight days, and here you are kicking up all this fuss. Many of the people here have been well for three weeks and look how patient they are!"

However, soon after this they did discharge me and I returned home. My wife said:

"Do you know, Petya, a week ago I thought you had passed over to a better world, for a notice came from the hospital saying: "Upon receipt of the present kindly apply immediately for your husband's body."

It turned out that my wife rushed to the hospital, but there they just said they were sorry and there had been some mistake in their book-keeping. Someone else had died and for some reason they imagined it might be me, although at that time I was quite well except for the nervous rash. Altogether this little incident created quite an unfavourable impression on me, and I felt like going to the hospital and swearing at someone, but when I thought of all the things that can happen in a place of that kind I decided it would be best not to go.

Now whenever I am ill I stay at home.

MIKHAIL ZOSHCHENKO

THE DISCERNING DOG

JEREMY BABKIN, that's the merchant who lives in our block of flats, had his fur coat pinched—a raccoon-lined overcoat it was—so he was regular cut up about it and didn't half carry on.

"Citizens," he says to us, " it's a mighty fine coat and no mistake. I regret losing it," he says, " so I'm sparing no expense till I catch the criminal and bash his face in! "

So Babkin applies for one of them criminal police-dogs. Well, a 'tec comes along presently in a peaked cap, legs in puttees and a dog along of him—a whopping, brownish, snoopy-looking hound—not at all the sort of dog you'd take to.

This 'tec leads the dog up to the door, sticks its head down to some foot-prints, says " Pst " and steps aside. The dog raises its head, sniffs the air, gives the crowd the once over—naturally we was all of us there by now—and makes straight for Fyokla from Number Five and sniffs at her skirt. The old woman edges into the crowd, but the dog grabs hold of her dress. She tries to get away, but the dog isn't having any : it hangs on to her skirt and won't let go.

Poor old Fyokla flops down on her knees before the 'tec.

" Me sins have found me out," she says; " I'm not denying nothing. Five buckets of illicit spirits, that's me, and the still—that's me too. You'll find everything in me bathroom," she says, " and I'll come to the police-station quietly."

All of us just gasps.

" But the fur coat," says Fyokla, " that's not me. I know nothing about no fur coat. But the other stuff—

that's me all right, so you can take me to the police. Hanging's too good for me!" she hollers.

So they lead her away, and the 'tec takes his hound back to the door, holds its nose down to the foot-marks and tells it to get on with it. Again the dog casts his eye over us, sniffs the air all around and this time picks on our house-warden. The warden goes pale and falls on the ground.

"Arrest me, good people, responsible citizens," he bawls. "I've collected the water-rate off you and spent it all on me own whims and pleasures."

Naturally the other tenants rush at the warden and start tying him up. Meanwhiles the dog is after the bloke from Number Seven and nips him by his trousers. Number Seven turns pale and falls down before the crowd.

"Guilty," he says. "I'm a guilty man all right. The year of me birth on me Labour Identity Card isn't right," he says, "'cos I've altered it. A fine, healthy young man like me—I should be in the Army defending me native land, and here I am, living at Number Seven, consuming electric power and enjoying other communal amenities. Arrest me!"

The crowd gets fidgety: the dog sort of gives them the creeps.

Meanwhiles Babkin himself blinks his eyes, takes a look round, fishes some money out of his pocket and hands it to the 'tec.

"Here," he says. "You take that hound of yours to the devil. If me raccoon coat's gone, it's gone, and there's an end to it. To hell with it!" he says.

But the dog's too quick for him. There it is wagging its tail at him. Babkin don't feel too good and moves away a bit, but the dog's after him all right, sniffing his galoshes. Babkin turns white as a sheet.

"Well, if it's like that there's no hiding the truth," he says. "I'm a blackguard all right, and as for that raccoon coat, chums, if I tell you the plain truth, it ain't mine: I pinched it off me own brother! Here I am, chums, sobbing me heart out!"

Well, after this the crowd just scatters right and left, and the dog don't have time to sniff the air any more; it just grabs the two or three citizens which comes handiest. All of them owns up. One says he's been playing cards and lost money that weren't his own; the second says he biffed his wife with a flat-iron; the third—well, what he says I don't even like to repeat.

So now there's no one left in the whole courtyard except the dog and the 'tec. And now the hound ups to the 'tec and wags its tail; he turns pale and falls on his knees:

"Bite me, canine citizen," he says to the dog. "I'm issued thirty roubles for your grub and keep twenty for myself!"

What happened after that I don't know: "Scram while the going's good" is my motto.

ISAAK BABEL

THE KING

WHEN the wedding-ceremony was over, the rabbi sat for a while in an armchair; then, going outside, he viewed the tables arrayed all down the courtyard. There were so many of them that those right at the end even poked out into Hospital Street. Velvet-spread, they wound their way down the yard like so many serpents with variegated patches on their bellies; and they sang full-throatedly, those patches of velvet, orange and red.

The living-quarters had been turned into kitchens. A sultry flame beat through the soot-swathed doorways,

a flame drunken and puffy-lipped. The faces of the
old crones broiled in its smoky rays; old women's
tremulous chins and beslobbered bosoms. Sweat with
the pinkness of fresh blood, sweat as pink as the slaver
of a mad dog, streamed this way and that over those
mounds of exorbitant and sweetly pungent flesh. Not
counting the washers-up, three old cooks were preparing
the wedding-feast; and supreme over all the cooks and
washers-up reigned the octogenarian Reisl, tiny and
hump-backed, as patina'd with tradition as a roll of the
Torah.

Before the feast began, a young man unknown to the
guests made his dim and elusive way into the yard.
Wanted a word with Benya Krik. Led Benya Krik un-
obtrusively aside.

"Listen here, King," said the young man. "A word
in your ear. I'm from Aunt Hannah in Kostetskaya
Street."

"Right," said Benya Krik, alias the King. "Out
with it."

"Aunt Hannah told me to tell you that there's a new
police-captain down at the station."

"Knew that much day before yesterday," said Benya
Krik. "Go on."

"The captain's gone and gathered the whole lot
together and speechified."

"New brooms," said Benya Krik. "He's planning
a raid. Go on."

"Suppose you know, King, when the raid will be."

"It's scheduled for tomorrow."

"For today, King."

"Who said so, young man?"

"Aunt Hannah. You know Aunt Hannah?"

"I do. Go on."

"The captain, I say, assembled all his men and made
a speech. We must settle Benya Krik's hash, he said,
seeing that where there's an emperor there's no room

for a king. Today, when Krik's sister's getting married
and they'll all be together, is just the day. We can nab
the lot."

"Go on."

"Well, the cops began to get windy. If we raid 'em
today, they said, on a day when Krik is celebrating, he'll
see red, and then blood will flow. So the captain said,
Duty before everything."

"Right. Off you go," said the King.

"What shall I tell Aunt Hannah?"

"Tell her: Benya knows all about the raid."

And so the young man departed. After him went
three of Benya's pals. Said they'd be back in half an
hour. And so they were.

Not according to their years did the wedding guests
take their seats. Foolish old age is no less pitiable than
timorous youth. Nor according to their wealth. Heavy
purses are lined with tears.

In the place of honour sat the bride and groom. Today
was their day. In the next place sat Zender Eichbaum,
father-in-law of the King. Such was his right. One
should know the story of Zender Eichbaum, for it is
no ordinary story.

How had Benya Krik, gangster and king of gangsters,
become Eichbaum's son-in-law? Become son-in-law of
a man who owned sixty milch-kine, all save one? The
answer lay in a foray. About a year before, Benya had
written Eichbaum a letter.

"Monsieur Eichbaum," he had written, "have the
goodness to deposit, tomorrow morning, in the entrance
to No. 17, Sofievskaya Street, the sum of twenty
thousand roubles. If you fail to comply with this request,
something unheard of will happen to you, and you will
be the talk of all Odessa. Yours respectfully, Benya the
King."

Three letters, each one more to the point than that
preceding, had remained unanswered. Then Benya

took steps. They came in the night, nine of them, bearing long poles in their hands. The poles were wrapped about with pitch-dipped tow. Nine flaming stars flared in Eichbaum's cattle-yard. Benya beat the locks from the door of the cowshed and began to lead the cows out one by one. Each was received by a lad with a knife. He would overturn the cow with one blow of the fist and plunge his knife into the vaccine heart. On the blood-flooded ground the torches bloomed like roses of fire. Shots rang out. With these shots Benya scared away the dairymaids who had come hurrying to the cowshed. After him other bandits began firing in the air. (If you don't fire in the air you may kill someone). And now, when the sixth cow had fallen, mooing her death-moo, at the feet of the King, into the graveyard in his underclothes galloped Eichbaum, asking:

"What good will this do you, Benya?"

"If I don't have my money, Monsieur Eichbaum, you won't have your cows. It's as simple as that."

"Come indoors, Benya."

And indoors they came to terms. The slaughtered cows were divided fairly between them, and Eichbaum was guaranteed the integrity of his possessions, even receiving a written pledge with affixed seal. But the wonder came later.

During the raid, on that dreadful night when cows bellowed as they were slaughtered and calves slipped and slithered in the blood of their dams, when the torch-flames danced like dark-visaged maidens and the farm-women lunged back in horror from the muzzles of amiable Brownings—on that dread night there ran out into the yard, wearing nought save her open-work shift, Tsilya the daughter of old man Eichbaum. And the victory of the King was turned to defeat.

Two days later, without warning, Benya returned to Eichbaum all the money he had taken from him; and then one evening he paid the old man a social call. He

wore an orange suit; beneath his cuff gleamed a bracelet
set with diamonds; he walked into the room, bowed
politely, and asked Eichbaum for his daughter's hand.
The old man had a slight stroke, but recovered. He was
good for another twenty years.

"Listen, Eichbaum," said the King. "When you die
I will bury you in the First Jewish Cemetery, right by
the entrance. I will raise you, Eichbaum, a monument
of pink marble. I will make you an Elder of the Brody
Synagogue. I will give up my own business and enter
yours as a partner. Two hundred cows we will have,
Eichbaum. I will kill all the other cow-keepers. No
thief shall walk the street you live in. I will build you
a villa where the tram-line ends. Remember, Eichbaum,
you were no rabbi in your young days. People have
forged wills, but why talk about it? And the King shall
be your son-in-law; no milksop, but the King."

And Benya Krik had his way; for he was passionate,
and passion rules the universe. The newly-weds spent
three months on the fat lands of Bessarabia, three months
flooded with grapes, rich food and the sweat of love's en-
counters. Then Benya returned to Odessa to marry off
his sister Deborah, a virgin of forty summers who
suffered from goitre. And now, having told the story
of Zender Eichbaum, let us return to the marriage of
Deborah Krik, sister of the King.

At the wedding-feast they served up turkey, roast
chicken, goose, stuffed fish, fish-soup in which lakes of
lemon gleamed nacrously. Over the heads of defunct
geese flowers swayed like luxuriant plumages. But does
the foamy surge of the Odessa sea cast roast chicken on
the shore?

All that is noblest in our smuggled goods, everything
for which the land is famed from end to end, did, on
that starry, that deep-blue night, its entrancing and
disruptive work. Wines not from these parts warmed
stomachs, made legs faint sweetly, bemused brains,

evoked belches that rang out sonorous as trumpets summoning to battle. The negro cook from the "Plutarch,"
that had put in three days before from Port Said, bore
unseen through the customs barrier fat-bellied jars of
Jamaica rum. oily Madeira, cigars from the plantations
of Pierpont Morgan and oranges from the environs of
Jerusalem. This is what the foaming surge of the Odessa
sea bears to the shore; this is what sometimes comes the
way of Odessa beggars at Jewish weddings. Jamaica
rum came their way at the wedding of Deborah Krik;
and so, having sucked their fill like infidel swine, the
Jewish beggars began to beat the ground deafeningly
with their crutches. Eichbaum, his waistcoat unbuttoned,
scanned with puckered eyes the tumultuous gathering,
hiccoughing lovingly the while. The orchestra played
a fanfare. It was just like a divisional parade: a fanfare
—nothing but. The gangsters, sitting in compact rows,
were at first excessively embarrassed by the presence of
outsiders; later they loosened up. Lyova the Butcher
cracked a bottle of vodka on the head of his beloved;
Monya the Gunner fired a shot in the air. The rejoicings
reached their pitch when, in accordance with the custom
of olden times, the guests began bestowing their
wedding-presents. One *shammes* from the Synagogue after
another leaped on a table and there, to the stormy wailing
of the fanfare, sang out how many roubles had been
presented, how many silver spoons. And now the
friends of the King showed what blue blood meant, and
the chivalry, not yet extinct, of the Moldavanka district.
On the silver trays, with ineffably nonchalant move-
ments of the hand, they cast golden coins, rings and
threaded coral.

Aristocrats of the Moldavanka, they were tightly en-
cased in raspberry waistcoats; russet jackets clasped their
shoulders, and on their fleshy feet the azure leather
cracked. Rising to their full height and thrusting out
their bellies, they beat their palms in time with the

music; with the traditional cry of " Bitter, bitter! " called
on the married couple to kiss, and showered the bride
in blossoms; and she, Deborah of forty summers, sister
of Benya Krik, distorted by her illness, with her swelling
crop and her eyes bulging from their orbits, sat on a pile
of cushions side by side with the feeble youth, now mute
with misery, whom Eichbaum's money had purchased.

The bestowal of gifts was drawing to a close, one
shammes after another was growing hoarse and croaky,
and the double-bass was at cross purposes with the fiddle.
Over the courtyard there suddenly spread a faint smell
of burning.

" Benya," said Papa Krik, famed among his fellow-
draymen as a bully, " Benya, d'you know what I think?
I think our chimbley's on fire."

" Papa," said Benya to his inebriated parent, " eat and
drink, and don't let such trifles bother you."

And Papa Krik followed the filial advice. Drink and
eat he did. But the smoke-cloud grew more and more
pungent. Here and there the edges of the sky were
turning pink, and now there shot up, narrow as a sword-
blade, a tongue of flame. The guests, half-rising from
their seats, began to snuffle the air, and the womenfolk
gave little squeaks of fear The gangsters eyed one
another. And only Benya Krik, aware of nothing, was
disconsolate.

" The celebration's going all to pieces," he cried, filled
with despair. " Good friends, I beg you, eat and drink! "

But now there appeared in the courtyard the same
young man as had come earlier in the evening.

" King," said he, " I'd like a word in your ear."

" Out with it, then," said the King. " I've always a
spare ear for a spare word."

" King," said the unknown young man, and giggled.
" It's really comical : the police-station's blazing like a
house on fire! "

The shopkeepers were silent. The gangsters grinned.

The sexagenarian Manka, ancestress of the suburban
bandits, placed two fingers in her mouth and whistled
so piercingly that her neighbours jerked away in fright.

"You're not on the job, Manka," observed Benya.
"More *sang-frwa!*"

The young man who had brought these astounding
tidings was still doubled up with laughter. He was chort-
ling like a schoolgirl.

"They came out of the station, forty of them," he
related, vigorously moving his jaws, "all set for the
raid; and they hadn't hardly gone fifty yards when the
whole place was on fire. Why don't you folks drop
round and watch it burn?"

But Benya forbade his guests to go and view the con-
flagration. He set out himself with two comrades. The
station was in a proper blaze. Policemen, their buttocks
waggling, were rushing up smoky staircases and hurling
boxes out of windows; the prisoners, unguarded, were
running riot. The firemen were filled with zeal, but
no water flowed when the nearest tap was turned.
The police-captain—the broom that was to have swept
clean—was standing on the opposite pavement; the ends
of his moustache curled into his mouth, and he was
biting them. Motionless the new broom stood there. As
he passed the captain, Benya gave him a military salute.

"Good health, Your Excellency," he said, deeply
sympathetic. "What do you say to this stroke of bad
luck? A regular act of God!"

He stared hard at the burning edifice and slowly shook
his head.

"Tut-tut-tut!" he went.

When Benya got back home the little lamps in the
courtyard were flickering out and dawn was beginning
to touch the sky. The guests had departed and the
musicians were dozing, leaning their heads on their
double-basses. Deborah alone was not thinking of sleep.

With both hands she was urging her faint-hearted husband towards the door of their nuptial chamber, glaring at him carnivorously. Like a cat she was, that holding a mouse in her jaws tests it lovingly with her teeth.

ILYA ILF - EVGENY PETROV

COLUMBUS REACHES THE SHORE

L AND, land!" joyfully cried the sailor, perched up on the mast-head.

The long voyage of Christopher Columbus, with its alarms and hazards, had come to an end. Land was in sight. Columbus seized his telescope with trembling hands.

" I see a large mountain range," said he to his shipmates, "but 'tis strange, there seem to be windows therein. Never before have I seen mountains with windows in them."

" A canoe with natives! " the cry resounded. Waving their ostrich-plumed hats, the discoverers of the new land, their cloaks sweeping behind them, rushed to the leeward deck.

Two natives in strange green garb climbed aboard and silently thrust before Columbus a large sheet of paper.

" I wish to discover your land," said Columbus proudly. " In the name of the Spanish Queen Isabella I declare these lands as belonging. . . ."

" Sure! But first fill up this questionnaire," said the native wearily. " Write in block capitals, your full name, nationality and family-circumstances, and declare whether or not you are suffering from trachoma, whether you are conspiring to overthrow the American Government, and whether or not you are an idiot."

Columbus grasped his sword. But as he did not happen to be an idiot, he at once calmed himself.

"One must not upset the natives," he said to his fellow voyagers. "Natives are like children. They sometimes have strange customs. I know this from experience."

"Have you a return ticket and five hundred dollars?" continued the native.

"And may I ask what are dollars?" asked the great seafarer with astonishment.

"You indicated right now in the questionnaire that you are not an idiot, yet you ask what a dollar is. What do you want to do here?"

"I want to discover America."

"And are you having any *publicity?*"

"*Publicity?*" I have never heard the word before."

The native looked at Columbus with a long and penetrating gaze and finally said:

"You don't know what *publicity* is?"

"N—no."

"And you have made up your mind to discover America? I guess I wouldn't like to be in your boots, Mr. Columbus."

"What do you mean? You think I shall not succeed in discovering this rich and fertile land?" anxiously enquired the great man from Genoa.

But the native had already gone away muttering under his breath: "You can't have prosperity without publicity."

By this time the caravels had reached the harbour. Autumn in these latitudes was beautiful. The sun shone and a gull circled astern. Deeply moved, Columbus set foot on the new land, holding in one hand a small parcel of beads which he intended to exchange at a profit for gold and ivory, and in the other an enormous Spanish flag. But no matter where he looked, nowhere was there the earth, grass or trees to which he was accustomed in peaceful old Europe. Everywhere he saw stone, asphalt,

cement, steel.

A huge crowd of people flowed past him with pencils, notebooks and cameras in their hands. They were crowding around a famous wrestler who had just disembarked from a nearby ship—a gentleman with flattened ears and an incredibly thick neck. No one paid the slightest attention to Columbus. Only two native women with painted faces came along.

" Who's that guy with the flag?" one of them asked.

" I guess it's an advertisement for a Spanish restaurant," replied the other. And they too hurried off to look at the gentleman with the flattened ears.

Columbus did not succeed in erecting the flag on American soil. To do that a preliminary boring operation with a pneumatic drill would have been necessary.

He had already tried picking a hole in the pavement with his sword, until it broke. So he was compelled to walk through the streets with the heavy gold-embroidered flag. Fortunately he no longer had to carry the beads. They had been confiscated at the customs.

Hundreds of thousands of natives hurried about their business, burrowed under the ground, ate, drank, traded, but never suspected that they had been discovered. Columbus meditated with bitterness: " I strive my utmost, I acquire money for this expedition, I cross the stormy ocean, I risk my life—and nobody pays the slightest attention to me."

He went up to a native who seemed to have a pleasant face and said proudly:

" I am Christopher Columbus."

" What's that you say? "

" Christopher Columbus."

" Spell it," said the native impatiently. Columbus spelled it.

" I guess I recollect something," replied the native; " you don't deal in portable machinery? "

" I discovered America," said Columbus impatiently.

" You don't say! Was it long ago? "

" No; just now, some five minutes ago."

" That's mighty interesting. And what is it you really want, Mr. Columbus?"

"I think," said the great seafarer modestly, " I think that I have the right to a certain amount of recognition."

" But didn't anyone meet you when you landed?"

" Nobody met me. It seems that the natives did not realise that I had come to discover them."

" You should have sent a cable. You can't go on like that! If you set about discovering a new land you should send a wire in advance, write down a few jokes to distribute to the reporters, and bring hundreds of photographs of yourself. The way you've been going on, you'll get nowhere. You need publicity."

" That is the second time I have heard that strange word *publicity*. What is it? Is it some religious rite, some heathen sacrifice?"

The native looked pityingly at this foreigner. " Surely you know that, Mr. Columbus," he said; " *publicity*— well I guess it's just publicity. I'll try to do something for you. I guess I'm sorry for you."

He took Columbus to a hotel and installed him on the thirty-fifth floor. Then he left him alone in his room, explaining that he would try to do something for him.

After half an hour the door opened and into the room walked the good native, accompanied by two others. One of them was chewing something all the time, while the other briskly set up a tripod, fixed a camera on it and said:

" Smile! Laugh! Now! Don't you get it? Well, do this: ' Ha-ha-ha,' and the photographer, with the skill of an expert, bared his teeth and began to neigh like a horse.

Christopher Columbus' nerves could not stand it and he began to laugh hysterically. There was a flash, the shutter clicked and the photographer said: " Thanks a lot."

Then the second native came up to Columbus and, without interrupting his chewing, took out a pencil and said :

" What's your surname?"

" Columbus."

" Spell it. C-O-L-U-M B U S? That's fine. It's mighty important not to get the name wrong. How long ago was it that you discovered America, Mr. Coleman? To-day? That's fine. How do you like America?"

" Well, you see, I have not yet seen enough of this fertile land to give judgment."

The reporter went into deep thought.

" Very well, then tell me, Mr. Coleman, what are the four things you like best in New York?"

" Well, you see, it is difficult. . . ."

The native again became submerged in deep thought. He was used to interviewing boxers and film-stars, and he found it difficult to deal with such a slow and dull type as Columbus. At last after summoning up all his resources he managed to think out a new and original question :

" Well, tell me, Mr. Columbus, two things which you do *not* like about New York."

Columbus gave forth a terrible sigh. Nothing so dreadful had ever happened to him before. He wiped the sweat from his brow and timidly asked his native friend :

" Perhaps after all I could get along somehow without *publicity?* "

" You're crazy," said the good native, turning pale. " The fact that you've discovered America—well it means nothing. What is important is that America should discover *you.*"

The reporter then made a gigantic mental effort. the result of which was the following extravagant question :

" How do you like American girls?"

Without waiting for a reply he began to write rapidly.

Every now and then he took a lighted cigarette from his mouth and stuck it behind his ear. Into his mouth thus vacated he placed his pencil and looked at the ceiling as if inspired. Then he began writing again. Finally he said " O.K.", patted the disconcerted Columbus on the back, shook him by the hand and went off.

" Well, now everything's set," said his native friend; " let us go for a stroll in the city. Now that you've discovered the country you must have a look at it. Only you can't take that flag into Broadway. Leave it in your room."

The walk down Broadway ended in a visit to a thirty-five cent burlesque from which the great and bashful Christopher ran like a scalded cat. He hurried swiftly through the streets, brushing the passers-by with his cloak and praying in a loud voice. Having attained his apartment he immediately threw himself on to the bed and, to the rumbling of the overhead railway, fell into a deep sleep.

Early next morning Columbus' patron rushed in triumphantly waving a newspaper. On the eighty-fifth page the seafarer saw with horror his own grinning physiognomy. Beneath was written that he was crazy about American girls, and that he considered them the most elegant women in the world; that he was the best friend of the Ethiopian Negus Selassie and moreover had decided to study geography at Harvard University.

The noble citizen of Genoa was about to open his mouth in order to swear that he had never said such things, when some new visitors appeared. They lost no time over polite formalities but came straight to the point. Publicity had begun to demonstrate its magical qualities: Columbus was invited to Hollywood.

" Mr. Columbus," explained the new visitors, " we want you to play the lead in an historical film, 'Amerigo Vespucci.' Do you get the idea? Christopher Columbus himself in the rôle of Amerigo Vespucci—it could be

mighty interesting. The public will flock to see such a
film. The main thing about the part is that the dialogue
will be spoken in Broadway jargon. Do you get me?
You don't? Then we'll explain right now in detail.
We have the scenario. It was made for the film of
Dumas' 'Count of Monte Cristo,' but that doesn't
matter; we've introduced elements bearing on the dis-
covery of America."

Columbus started to reel and silently began moving
his lips, obviously praying. But one of the natives from
Hollywood boldly continued:

" So, Mr. Columbus, you will play the part of Amerigo
Vespucci with whom the Spanish Queen is madly in
love. He, for his part, is madly in love with a Russian
Princess Grishka.* But Cardinal Richelieu bribes Vasco
da Gama and with the help of Lady Hamilton gets you
sent to America. His hellish plan is clear enough. You
are attacked by pirates on the high seas. You fight like a
lion. The scene runs to three hundred metres of film.
It's true you don't know how to act but that doesn't
matter."

" What does matter, then? " groaned Columbus.

"Publicity, Mr. Columbus. You are now known to
the public, and they will be mighty interested to see how
such an esteemed and learned man fights with pirates.
It ends with your discovering America, but that's of
no consequence. The chief thing is the fight with the
pirates. You get the idea, Mr. Columbus? Halberds,
battle-axes, catapults, Greek fire, yataghans,—we've got
all that mediæval stuff. Only you'll have to shave. No
beards and moustaches. The public has already seen so
many in films about Russian life that it just can't stand
any more. So you shave right now and then we sign a
contract for six weeks. Agreed?"

" O.K." said Columbus, trembling from head to foot.

* Grishka is the familiar form of a man's name—the Russian equivalent
of Gregory.

Late that evening he sat at a table and penned this letter to the Queen of Spain:

"*I have sailed many seas but never before have I met with such original natives. They cannot bear quietness, and in order the more often to enjoy noise have constructed special roads through the town on iron columns along which iron chariots whirl day and night, producing the rumbling so well-beloved of the natives.*

Whether they practise cannibalism I have not yet ascertained with certainty, but at all events they certainly eat hot dogs. I have seen with my own eyes many an eating-house where passers-by are invited to partake of hot dogs, the taste of which is highly praised.

Everyone here smells of a peculiar scent which in the native tongue is called 'Gasoline.' All the streets

are filled with this aroma, which is very unpleasant to the European sense of smell. Even the young women here smell of it. I have established the opinion that the natives are heathens: they have many gods, the names of which are written in light on their huts. They appear to worship most of all the goddess Coca Cola, the god Druggist Soda, the goddess Cafeteria, and the great god of the gasoline aromas—Ford. The latter here appears to perform the function of Zeus.

The natives are very gluttonous and chew the whole time.

Unfortunately civilisation has not yet touched them. In comparison with the furious tempo of contemporary life in Spain the life of the Americans is extremely slow. Even walking on foot seems to them an excessively rapid means of locomotion. In order to slow up this process they have instituted an enormous number of so-called 'automobiles.' On these they ride one behind the other at a snail's pace through the town, and this pleases them in great measure.

I have been struck by a certain ceremony in the place known as 'Broadway.' A large number of natives gather together in a large hut called a 'burlesque.' Several native women mount up on a raised platform and, to the barbaric sound of tom-toms and saxophones, begin removing their clothes. Those present clap their hands like children. When the last woman is almost naked and the natives in the hall have reached the highest pitch of excitement, something quite inconceivable happens in this amazing ceremony: the curtain goes down and the spectators disperse to their dwellings.

I hope to continue the investigation of this remarkable country and to penetrate into the interior of the continent. The natives are very kind and hospitable, and are well disposed towards strangers."

Book 10
voiceless
th

Phonics Reading Program 2

Sloth Sleuth

by Quinlan B. Lee

SCHOLASTIC INC.

New York   Toronto   London   Auckland   Sydney
Mexico City   New Delhi   Hong Kong   Buenos Aires

We need to find Sammy the **Sloth.**
Do you **think** you can help us?

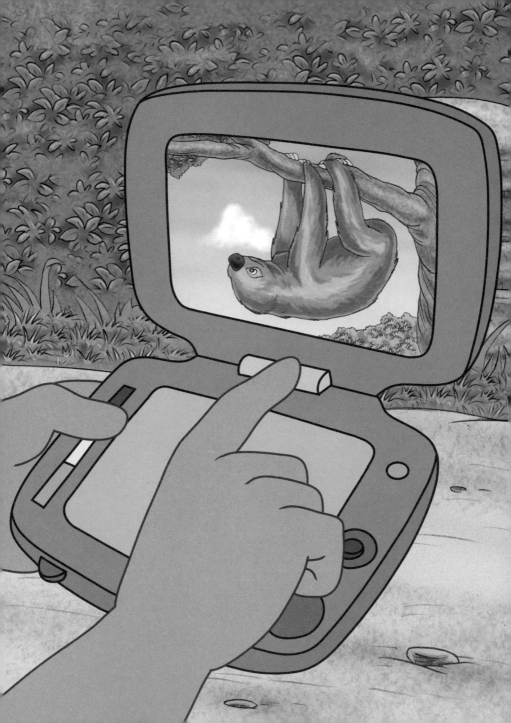

Sloths live in trees.
Sloths have **three** toes.
Here is the **path.**
Let's go!

Look by the **path**!
I see **three** toes.
Is it Sammy the **Sloth?**

It has **three** toes.
But it is not a **sloth.**
Sloths live in trees.
It is a tapir.

Keep on the **path.**
Look up!
I **think** I see toes.

Is it a **three**-toed **sloth**?
No, it is a tree frog.
Tree frogs have four **thin**
toes.

Look. I see **three** toes in
a tree.
One, two, **three.**
Do you **think** it is a **sloth?**

It is a **sloth** in the tree. **Thanks** for helping us find Sammy!